ALSO BY THOMAS PRIDE

Fever

King and Country

The Baron

Wonderful Untouchables

Zayed

Mercia

THOMAS PRIDE

Ucadia Books Company

The greatest of stories & legends

Few stories are better loved or known than the tale of King Arthur and the Knights of the Round table. Since the first published story about an ancient king known as Arthur (more than 800 years ago) by Geoffrey of Monmouth, the world has been fascinated by the legends surrounding a virtuous king, against the forces of evil. Yet, what if the real story - the true story - is vastly more compelling and exciting than the mythical quests and magical swords of countless books and movies?

What if the true story of Artur of the Pendraig reveals a moment in time at the end of the Dark Ages, when the future of Christianity in Western Europe hung in the balance? When former foes became unlikely allies in a fierce battle against forces seeking to keep a people divided by any means? What if the biggest hidden secret to Artur of Pendraig is him being the first true Christian King of Britain?

Mercia is a powerful and gripping epic that finally removes the veil that has for too long hidden the real and historic figures of Artur of Pendraig and Pengwern (Shrewsbury), Gwynedd (Lancelot) of Angels (Angelsea) and Hollyhead, Gwenhwyfawr of Gwent and Casnewydd, Myrddin of Glastonbury and Morgannag of Glywysing and Caerdyf (Cardiff).

To my mother Stephanie and father Glynn.

Then you will know the truth, and the truth will set you free.

John 8:32

Chapter 1

The stone face of a carved figure upon a tomb was momentarily illuminated by the flickering and dancing flames from several torches. Wise, firm and ancient; the figure was abruptly obscured by a white sheet, as multiple hands frantically began rubbing red coloured ochre into the paper. Slowly and methodically, the image of the stone face re-appeared onto the paper sheet along with the image of a noble woman beside him.

Only then, once the entire detail of a magnificent tomb had finally appeared onto the paper, did the last of the frantic hands rubbing the ochre cease. An intricate carving of a King and Queen holding hands, both in full armour and dress, with ancient Gaelic writing below:

"Pray thee Pilgrim for the noble souls of Artur and Gwenhwyfawr, united once more here in peace. First King of all Great Britain. First faithful servant of the Vicar of Christ and Universal Church. Let all men who seek rule, be measured according to thy virtue."

The hands of the men who had just etched the stone carving release their grip. The paper was then pulled away from the sacred tomb revealing the stone face itself once again.

There was the sound of men mumbling in the background, then silence, before a set of iron bars began to violently strike the face of the tomb. Within moments it started to crack and split into pieces.

The faces and dress of the men who had just destroyed the tomb are revealed. They are dressed in the classic colours of the State of Venice, with plumed helmets and multi-coloured vests. Dozens more Venetian Mercenaries hold monks stripped down to their white under garments lined up and kneeling in front of the backdrop of an intact Glastonbury Abbey. To the side, a handful of mercenaries oversee other monks being forced at the point of blades to ferry manuscripts across to feed a ferocious bonfire of burning treasures. Such were the events in the year 1536.

On horseback overseeing the scene of carnage and destruction was a sharp faced man (Francesco Zorzi) in magnificent gold silks, alongside the unmistakable figure of King Henry VIII.

Henry appeared visibly uneasy at the scene before them, looking over to Zorzi.

"Do we really have to do this?" sighed the King.

Chapter 1

"The truth is a blinding mirror, your Majesty,"replied Zorzi. "Smash the past and you shall become master of your own destiny."

King Henry huffed as he shook his head, staring at the broken pieces of the tomb.

"Do you mean the great Arthur?" asked Zorzi sarcastically. He allowed himself a brief laugh before continuing, "your majesty. He was no hero. He murdered my ancestors just as he murdered yours, remember?"

A Venetian mercenary approached, interrupting Zorzi and saluted. "We have searched everywhere and have not found it, sir."

Zorzi let the words sit for a moment as he continued to survey the horror before him. He looked over at his troops holding the monks in a line, waiting diligently for his command and then returned to focusing back on the soldier in front of his horse.

"Destroy it! Destroy it all!"

With that, the soldier saluted and scampered back toward an awaiting troop holding torches near the buildings and bonfire. Zorzi then turned to view the slumped figure of Henry VIII, desperate to look away.

"Your grief will soon pass your majesty. Upon this sacrifice we will build a new faith and a new world order, with you as the first and greatest of all kings."

Zorzi then turned his attention to the troops holding the monks in a line. A hand signal across the neck was all Zorzi needed to do. With that one simple gesture sixty swords were raised in unison above the heads of the monks.

****

Pengwern (Shrewsbury), Kingdom Of Pendraig, 865 CE.

The exhausted and bloodied face of resignation was plain to see, as the young Artur Pendraig knelt among a line of prisoners. The dull thud of a sword in the background, until the sight of the bloodied sword moved into position in front of the face of Artur, momentarily catching a glint of sunlight.

Pulling back, a chaotic scene was revealed of an ancient courtyard following the aftermath of battle. A scattering of sobbing women and children tending the injured and removing the dead. Imposing Norman Guards stood at strategic positions as smoke billowed overhead from fires still smouldering.

At the centre of the courtyard was Artur kneeling midst a bloody scene as nearby bodies were dragged away. Behind Artur was a giant Norman Swordsman. To the side a Deacon holding a large cross was shouting prayers.

In front of this scene were two figures, one being the semi-conscious Uther Pendraig slumped on the stone of the courtyard between two Norman guards. The other lying on a wood and fur bed, being the unconscious and pale Ragnar Lodbrok, surrounded by half a dozen Norman bodyguards.

"May the Alpha and Omega have mercy on your heathen soul," yelled the Deacon at Artur.

The Deacon made the sign of the cross at Artur as the giant Norman Swordsman raised his sword about to strike. At that moment there was a shout as Ubbe Ragnarsson entered the courtyard.

"Halt!"

Immediately the Norman swordsman withdrew his sword and the Deacon leapt back, startled by the booming one word command. The voice was powerful enough voice to wake the dying Ragnar.

"My Lord, they are heretics against Christ for which the law commands death," the Deacon protested.

"Take care of your words deacon," responded Ubbe. "No man is immune to the law. Especially one such as you who takes it upon himself to be judge and executioner of women and children."

Ubbe walked quickly toward Ragnar Lodbrok and signalled to the Norman guards, pointing at the Deacon. The Norman guards immediately pressed forward and seized the Deacon.

"But my Lord," screeched the Deacon. "I represent the See of Antioch."

Artur remained kneeling in front of the giant Swordsman, while Ubbe waved his hand to the Norman guards to remove the Deacon. Even as he was being dragged away, the Deacon continued screeching his authority.

Ubbe gently kneeled before Ragnar Lodbrok and started to sob. Ragnar reached out with a bloodied arm to touch the face of Ubbe.

"A heavy toll be this Divine Mission, my son," coughed Ragnar. "Give unto your brothers Ivar and Halfdane my blessings."

"Father, I have summonsed our best healers," replied Ubbe. "Resist the calls of heaven and let me tend to your wounds."

Ragnar pointed his frail bloodied arm at the forlorn figure of Uther Pendraig, bloodied and propped up across the room.

"My son, we are Soldiers of Christ, not barbarians," he cried.

Ubbe nodded and looked over to his guards.

"Quickly, " said Ubbe, pointing to Uther Pendraig, "get some bedding for Uther."

The Norman guards hurry away.

"My son," continued Ragnar, "these men fought with honour. Promise you shall not be a tyrant. Let men of honour be ...men."

"Father!"

Ragnar drew his last breath, before the air of his lungs exhaled on their own accord. Ubbe grabbed hold of Ragnar and embraced him in terrible grief as the Norman guards returned and lifted Uther Pendraig into a similar wooden frame with bedding and skins.

Ubbe continued to embrace his dead father, as he looked over at Artur, still kneeling and signalled to the guards.

"Release him."

Mercia

Artur got to his feet and bowed slowly to Ubbe, before moving over to kneel before Uther, embracing him by the arm. Artur looked back at Ubbe, distraught with grief.

"As my father bound me," said Ubbe, "I shall spare your life. We both be orphans today."

Ubbe Ragnarsson slowly picked himself up and bowed to Artur, who acknowledged Ubbe again, as Norman bodyguards picked up the body of Ragnar Lodbrok.

"I shall call on you soon," added Ubbe. "Do not test my faith that we must make more widows."

The Norman guards departed carrying the body of Ragnar, followed by Ubbe, with his head bowed, shuffling behind. Except for the few women and children and the dead, Artur was now alone with Uther.

"Luki, the god of good fortune smiled on you today my son," Uther wheezed in pain.

"Few others did they favour," said Arthur. "We lost...I have lost too much. "

"So did the Normans and Ragnarsson," replied Uther, before coughing up blood.

"Enough," cried Artur. "Let me get a healer to tend to you."

"Save your breath. Where I go, I shall soon be with your mother, your brothers, your wife and your son."

"Father please. You cannot go. I forbid it. What shall we do? How shall we overcome?"

"What you have always done."

"Promise me."

"Father, please save your strength."

"Artur Pendraig promise to me you will keep your sacred word."

"I promise," replied Artur, his voice quivering in grief.

"Then my son, you have nothing to fear."

Uther closed his eyes and faded away, as Artur embraced him, sobbing uncontrollably.

****

Beside the entrance to a great mound of stone, stood Artur, flanked by half a dozen druids in ceremonial red garments. They watched a slow procession of bodies being placed within the tomb. Behind them, a throng of people stood at a respectful distance.

Alwyn, the most senior of the druids, placed his hand on the shoulder of Artur as comfort. Yet Artur stood emotionless, as if carved of stone.

Mercia

"My Lord Artur, the gods must surely have a plan," said Alwyn softly.

Artur remained mute as the body of his deceased wife was brought forward to be interred.

"Our beloved Queen, your wife, neither suffered nor was disgraced."

The body of the son of Artur then passed by on its way to the tomb.

"What then is this mysterious plan of the Gods that you speak? Here my son here Amar. I could not even recognise his face after fire had done its worst!" Artur shook his head at the druid. "Why does everything have to be the plan of the gods? If that be true, then I am much tempted to disavow all of them."

"Lord Artur please," cried Alwyn. "For their sake and their journey, I beg you respect custom."

"What is custom then Druid? Why cannot you people give people straight answers," snapped Artur. "The will of the Gods is not an answer. It is an excuse for lack of true knowledge."

"My Lord you are deep in grief," protested Amar.

"And the custom you so dearly speak makes no sense. Then do not speak to me of gods or their plans again Alwyn," growled Artur as he followed behind the last body as it entered the tomb.

Chapter 1

At the entrance, Artur turned and held his hand at the druids following him.

"Let me grieve in peace."

The druids stopped and bowed as the figure of Artur disappeared inside the tomb.

Mercia

Chapter 2

Lindor (Lincoln), Capital of Norman Cambria, England

Artur and a small troop approached the main gate to the Lindor Castle. A set of decaying bodies in priestly robes hung in iron gibbets from the battlements. One of them had the same vestments as the Deacon, but was otherwise unrecognisable.

Artur and his troop entered into the castle courtyard and dismounted, handing their horses to the Norman guards. One giant of a man, (Ivar Olik) stepped forward to greet them.

"Artur of the Pendraig?"

Artur nodded affirmatively and Ivar then pointed in the direction of a large set of guarded doors leading from the courtyard.

"Please follow me."

Artur and his men follow Ivar through the doors and then the corridors until they enter the main hall.

Seated in a high ceiling hall, surrounded by guards was Ubbe Ragnarsson, with three wolf hounds sitting at his feet.

Mercia

When Artur entered, the dogs stood up and lumbered over to sniff Artur and his men. Artur extended his open left hand to the dogs.

"They like you," smiled Ubbe. "Most people are terrified by them. My brother Ivar gave them to me as a present from the Sacred Island."

Artur patted the dogs as he moved closer to Ubbe, while his men remained at a distance. "They are handsome," he replied.

As Artur approached, Ubbe got up from his chair to greet him, embracing his arm.

"Artur, I pray you trust my word when I say I had nothing to do with the death of your wife or your son. Yet I have punished those who did."

Artur nods, "Yes, I saw that on the entrance to the castle."

Ubbe shook his head. "Fanatics," he moaned. "They convince themselves of their own moral superiority and that their twisted notion of faith permits them to do all kinds of evil."

Ubbe looked over at Artur who seemed at pain on the subject. Ubbe then signalled Artur to follow him toward a great map on the side wall. It was a huge detailed map of the Western and Northern world, with remarkable accuracy for latitude and longitude.

Chapter 2

"Have you ever seen such a map before Artur of Pendraig?"

Artur shook his head. "Never," he said. "I did not think such wisdom existed?"

Ubbe smiled as Artur now stood beside him. "It comes from the ancients. Our ancestors saved a much smaller copy and I had this larger map made. Do you know much about our history?"

"A little," replied Artur.

"We come from the great North land, or Nor land you see here," said Ubbe whilst pointing with a stick to a remarkable likeness of Greenland, but without glaciers. "Three hundred years ago, it was still a land twenty times the size of this island, but full of people, of life, of animals and joy. But then the gods you still worship abandoned us. After the cold, came the famine and then the great sickness."

"I have heard of the great sickness," said Artur.

"Nothing but death. Our people were forced to flee for their own survival. The first were with Dan and then his son Herogar. They are the founders of Daneland. They are the ones that expelled the Persian Moors who call themselves the Amoricans, back to their island of Wex."

Ubbe turned away from the map and picked up a cross on a side table and then continued,

"But the biggest group found sanctuary under the Holly Christian King Gabran of Dal Riata under my ancestor Valdar, who swore a sacred oath to Christ not to worship or follow gods so cruel upon their people. So here we are. In lands where there is plenty of space for all to live peacefully."

"Yet you war with those few people," replied Artur. "You kill innocent women and children."

"I, Ubbe Ragnarsson am a Servant of Christ, not a murderer of innocents," growled Ubbe. "As I said to you, religious fanatics and ignorant men possessed by madness kill women and children."

Ubbe softened his tone. "Artur, it grieves me the loss of your family, the loss of your wife Eadythe. Yet I did not kill your son Amar. And as you saw, those responsible have been punished."

An awkward silence, before Artur spoke in reply. "How then do you account for Halfdane your brother?"

Ubbe allowed himself a brief smile. "You are correct Artur that my brother Halfdane can be cruel. Yet it is your people who refuse to live peacefully. Verily, before we even came, you were warring amongst yourselves; and now that we are here, only sometimes do your tribes unite to fight. My brother Ivar rebuilt Dublin, after your own King Máel Sechnaill burnt it to the ground, killing so many innocent women and children.”

“I am Artur Pendraig of the Dragon Clan. Neither my House nor my allies are like such people.”

“That is why I spared you,” said Ubbe. “That is why my father demanded before he died that I honour your courage and speak with you as a man and not as some savage.”

Ubbe moved over to another map on a table, showing drawings and plans.

“The heathen tribes to the south cannot be trusted. It is why I am building a wall of five great forts to protect us from Stamfor in the east, then Ligor, Tamwor, Hambor and Herefor to the West. But you Artur and the tribes to the west fight like men, not weasels.”

“I respect your good faith and conscience Lord Ubbe. But, even if it means death, I cannot abandon my honour to the law of Tara and the ancient gods.”

“That is why I wish to honour you Artur. No deacons, no demand to pledge to Christ. You shall be my shield in the west as the people of Mercia and I shall be your teacher of what our people have learned of restoring civilisation and prosperity."

"You honour me, more than I deserve Lord Ubbe. But even to fight for you under your flag would be a betrayal of my oath foresworn."

"Then do it for your united people of Mercia. If you hold the west, I shall not call upon you in my troubles. I promise this now. But I shall not beg. Nor shall I make such entreats again."

"Then I pledge my fealty, my men, my house and my life to honouring this covenant and to the creation of Mercia."

"Surely, there be no spirit or god in heaven that does not shine upon thee today Artur Pendraig."

****

Carmarthen, Capital of Dyfed, South Wales

The majestic heights of an ancient fort town, by a river cove. Upon the highest parapet fluttered the flags and colours of those kings in residence. Moving closer, the largest of these flags was the unmistakable Welsh dragon of Artur of Pendraig.

Chapter 2

Within a dimly lit cavernous hall, a fierce debate echoed. Around a long table were seven Kings seated, including Artur Pendraig, Cyngen of Powys, Osmond of Wicce, Gwgon of Ceredig, Owell of Glywysing, Gwythyr of Gwent and the host Bleddri Of Dyfed.

"No one is doubting your virtue Artur," continued Gwgon of Ceredig. "If it were I, then I would have thrust a lethal blow into the Norman beast. But to entreat with such monsters?"

Owell of Glywysing nodded in agreement. "Hear, hear," he added against the background of continued mumbling.

"Artur, you know the tribes of Wicce remain steadfast in our honour to such ancient accords with the Pendraig," said Osmond of Wicce. "Indeed, we have all lost one we love. Nor could anyone blame you for pursuing peace. But at what cost?"

Artur raised his hand and waited for silence to return. "My Lords and Kings, thank you for your counsel, your kindness and frankness," he smiled. "Yet none of what I have faithfully recounted from the truce of Ragnarsson be as an act of submission, but an opportunity of reason."

Artur then looked directly at each of the kings seated with him and said, "yet our clans and tribes have been fighting one another now for nearly four generations." He then looked at Cyngen of Powys.

"Tell me Cyngen of Powys, when can you recall in the records of your house a time of peace for more than one generation?"

Cyngen of Powys shook his head. Arthur then looked directly at Gwgon of Ceredig.

"Or you Gwgon of Ceredig. When has your kingdom ever experienced a lasting peace with your northern neighbors and with our host?"

"Because they be thieves of sheep and cattle," snarled Gwgon of Ceredig, causing Cyngen of Powys to stand up from his seat.

"I shall strike out your tongue for such insolence this instant," snapped back Cyngen of Powys at Gwgon of Ceredig.

Artur stood up from his seat, lowering his hands. "Now, my Lords. I entreat you to hear me first, without cause to arms against your fellow kings. For this be the sign of our malady. That even in unity of grief, our impulse to belligerence be our doom."

A brief and awkward silence until Owell of Glywysing spoke up.

"Artur, this may all be well and good," said Owell of Glywysing, "but Rhodri Mawr of the Angels be absent."

Chapter 2

"It is true," added Bleddri Of Dyfed. "Without him, we may well resolve to plant our heels. He carries the weight of many of the Holly priests."

"You may be Owain Bleddri of Dyfed," interjected Gwythyr of Gwent, "but let Artur of Pendraig finish his discourse."

Artur nodded at Gwythyr of Gwent in appreciation before continuing.

"I pray, each of you consider beyond those voices for whom our most sacred fields are full of stone epitaphs," said Artur. "And that it is the children of our clans who know nothing of peace, or art, or poetry, or reading. There be no honour in war without end. No virtue in the ignorance and waste of our people. This is what Ragnarsson pleads we consider through Mercia. Without demand of faith, or arms, or tribute. Just that we be men and defend what is ours."

All of the kings nodded their heads in agreement with the words of Artur, except Gwgon of Ceredig, who chimed in with his own doubts.

"Why? Why would Ubbe Ragnarsson offer such handsome terms?" asked Gwgon of Ceredig. "There must be a trick, a ruse, a purpose?"

"Why must there be?" responded Artur. "Are we so broken by battle that we no longer can see? We are not alone in a yearning for peace. Ragnarsson knows he cannot hold the centre if he must fight us and the south and east. "

"Then strike. Strike now," demanded Cyngen of Powys. "When Ragnarsson is not expecting and be rid of him, once and for all."

Gwythyr of Gwent laughed boisterously. "Less haste Cyngen of Powys," he chuckled. "Let our inevitable deaths be of at least some value and best choosing."

Gwgon of Ceredig shrugged his shoulders. "I see the logic of it Artur. I cannot speak for all the kings present but recognise my people are sorely in need of a moment to rebuild so much of what has been lost."

Osmond of Wicce nodded in agreement, saying "the Wicce honour our sacred pledge to the Pendraig and shall stand by your word and the formation of the covenant of Mercia. But what of Rhodri of the Angels?"

Artur let a moment pass and then smiled at the assembled kings. "If I can count on you men of honour to keep the peace amongst yourselves, then I shall visit Rhodri."

Chapter 3

Medina, Capital of Wex, Isle of White

A tall and narrow castle (the Fortress of Medina) gripped the foreshore. A high watchtower dominating its battlements, while stone docks radiated from its seaward foundations, like the arms of an octopus.

Set upon two of the stone docks were rows upon rows of iron cages, filled with forlorn and frightened children in chains. Alongside such an unholy cargo, a fleet of Moorish ships were tied up, loading the cages onboard.

Up in the watchtower within a surprisingly bright room, a man at one end (Æthelred) in an oversized cape, stood transfixed, admiring his own image reflected in a long mirror held by two nervous servants. Æthelred turned to the side, gesturing wildly as if practising the casting of spells, before turning to the other side and repeating the gestures.

Nearby, a scribe (Æthelweard) sat at a long bench, drowning in manuscripts, busily writing.

At the other end of the room, was a man (Ælfred) in bright flowing silks who watched on intently as a sculptor appeared to be desperately trying to finish a clay likeness of a young handsome half-naked boy wearing wings, standing frozen in fear.

The scribe (Æthelweard) stood up and began reciting.

"Alas, the King Æthelberht did die in the year of our Lord 865, having united the whole kingdom, and held it in good order and great tranquillity."

"Our brother was a pig," sniggered Ælfred as he continued to smile at the young boy with wings. "Why do you honour him so, in making him to be a king?"

"Posterity Ælfred," replied Æthelred sharply. "Something you are yet to comprehend beyond your obsession in playing with the live stock. "

"Sire does it sound to your liking?" asked Æthelweard to Ælfred, who continued to be besotted with his own image.

Æthelred nodded approvingly. "Yes, yes, it is fine. We just need to replace the ending. Order and tranquillity sounds too boring. Æthelweard we need something with more drama."

Ælfred started to laugh. "Brother you are wasting your time. My bronze statutes will outlast your fictions a hundred times longer."

"No brother it is you who are missing the big picture," grumbled Æthelred as he undid the cape and threw it at the servants holding the mirror, before pivoting around and walking over to his brother. "The Celt tribes have destroyed one another back to being illiterate savages. They have no memory of the truth of their heritage. Thus, it is we the Amoricans reborne as the House of Wex that shall be the only ones remembered."

A messenger entered the room and grovelled himself before the feet of Æthelred, thrusting the message above his head.

"My Lord, a message from Dyfed," the messenger mumbled, before Æthelred snatched the message from him and the messenger scurried away.

Æthelred started to read the message.

"What is it?" asked Ælfred.

"It seems that Artur of the House of Pendraig has consummated himself in matrimony unto to the Norman beast and formed a new alliance of tribes called Mercia."

Ælfred let out a cackling laugh.

"I fear not the Pendraig nor any of the Celts," he sniggered. "They are slow and dim witted."

"And you are boastful and foolish brother and not the Baal El of our family business," replied Æthelred condescendingly. "We are merchants. One celtic boy, especially if he be a eunuch fetches us from our Moor cousins more gold than a hundred sheep."

At this point, the young boy strung with wings, collapsed in fear and Ælfred rushed over to him.

"Fear not, He is not speaking of you, young man."

Ælfred reached into his pocket and produced several sweets.

"Here, would you like some sweets?"

The boy grabbed the sweets from Ælfred and began eating, as Ælfred glared back at Æthelred.

"Then other than insult, what do you say brother?"

"To use this new alliance of Artur as an opportunity to negotiate with the Danes," grinned Æthelred, "And in the process, gain ourselves a kingdom."

****

Holly Head, Capital of Angels Clan, Isle of Anglesey.

Artur and his troop of men directed their horses along a steep and narrow seaside approach to an open gate through heavy battlements (Holly head on Anglesey). They entered the protected town of Holly, before taking a steep path even higher to the main castle.

Chapter 3

Artur stopped at the outer walls and bridge to the castle, as the main gate to the castle was closed. Slowly, the gate opened, but before Artur and his soldiers could advance, a single young man on horse (Gwynedd) emerged from the castle, blocking their path.

"State your purpose," snapped Gwynedd.

"I am Artur of Pendraig. Here to seek audience with King Rhodri of the Angels. And who might you be?"

"I am Gwynedd, son of Rhodri. You are not welcome Artur of Pendraig."

"Is this your novel method of dispensing custom from the beginning of time, to deny hospitality and to rest our horses?"

From the parapets of the castle, the figure of Rhodri appeared.

"No, it is mine," shouted Rhodri. "Though my son be more than a match for all of you men. Your horses are welcome to rest. But you men can camp on the outskirts of town."

"My Lord," called out Artur. "I entreat that we might discuss the matter of events of the Norman and Ragnarsson."

"Artur of Pendraig, please excuse my disposition as I grieved for your father and for your loss. But though I am old, I am not deaf of hearing of your truce and proposed alliance of clans."

"But surely I shall be without voice soon, if we continue," yelled Artur. "Pray, you let us in to discuss."

"I shall not take arms against thee Pendraig, in memory of your father. Nor shall I seek arms, unless provoked against those who foolishly follow. Yet this is my final word, I shall not join thee in this union."

Artur lowered his head, then looked once more up at Rhodri.

"Very well. May the road rise up to greet you Rhodri Mawr and may ever the gods be in your favor."

Artur turned his horse and his men around and they departed.

****

London, Capital of Daneland, England

A dark, filthy and squalid settlement of stone, disease and squalor, scarcely modified in design since Roman (Londinium) times.

Æthelred and Ælfred, accompanied by a fierce cadre of bodyguards, entered ancient London (London) via the south gate from the Thames, as peasants and merchants paid no attention and continued about their lives. They turned left past the former Roman ruins of the forum, converted into a putrid sea of vices and perversions, from makeshift brothels and amateur surgeons, to soothsayers and public executions.

At the south gate to the ancient former Roman fort of London, Æthelred and Ælfred entered to meet King Guyhrum of Daneland.

Inside, Æthelred and Ælfred were confronted with the uncomfortable sight of King Guyhrum finishing relieving himself in a copper urn, held nervously by two attendants, in full view of his court, before his sorry attendants tip-toed away with the urn.

"What brings the Amoricans to Daneland?" bellowed King Guyhrum, as he adjusted his undergarments and sat back down on his chair.

"The events of the Celts truce with the Normans my lord," said Æthelred gently.

"I have no quarrel with Ubbe or Halfdane," grinned King Guyhrum.

"Yet, their truce with Artur of Pendraig unites the warring tribes for the first time as Mercia," replied Æthelred.

"So?" said King Guyhrum flippantly.

Æthelred struggled to keep his outward appearance of tranquillity.

"Is this not troubling?" he added, unable to contain himself.

The face of King Guyhrum hardened, before reddening with anger.

"Do not lecture me Amorican!" he yelled. "I do not wish to purchase your poisons, or debauch myself with your young livestock, or hire your assassins. Leave politics then to those men actually prepared to die in battle."

Æthelred bowed his head, trying his very best to appear humble. Ælfred stepped forward.

"We merely wish to help you Lord," said Ælfred soothingly. "We simply wish to help supplement your strength."

Æthelred looked up and nodded in agreement with his brother.

"It is true my Lord. The threat of a united Celtic kingdom is as much a threat to your kingdom as it is our business."

"The slavery business," interjected King Guyhrum sarcastically.

"For which you my Lord have been handsomely paid," replied Æthelred without emotion. "Verily, if the

Celts are united, then even our humble sanctuary of Wex, could be threatened. That is why we propose a truce."

"A truce?" asked King Guyhrum.

"We shall fund the import of a mercenary force to protect the west of your lands," continued Æthelred, "in exchange for our right to administer these lands on your behalf. Of course with a handsome reward."

"Why should I trust you?"

Æthelred bowed his head again before smiling at King Guyhrum.

"Truly your destruction would be our destruction. As you have so elegantly observed, we are but an ancient line of merchants. We have no task for battle ourselves, nor the sight of blood. Therefore this be for mutual survival."

A moment passed as Æthelred and Ælfred waited for the reply of King Guyhrum, as the king continued to rub his chin and contemplate.

****

Lindor (Lincoln) Castle, Cambria

Mercia

Artur and Ubbe Ragnarsson stood in front of a long table covered in maps and tables.

In the background, a sea of scribes, monks and scholars of all ages, watched on, whilst listening and diligently writing.

Ubbe Ragnarsson, signalled to one of the advisors (Wulfhere) to step forward. Wulfhere approached, carrying a green covered manuscript.

"Artur, this here is Wulfhere, our new Deacon and master scholar in Latin, Greek and Gaelic."

Wulfhere bowed to Artur. "My lord, a gift for your people," said Wulfhere as he bowed to Artur, before handing the manuscript to him. Artur nodded, before opening it up and viewing its pages.

Ubbe Ragnarsson, looked at Artur as he continued to look at the pages.

"I can see Artur, that you are indeed a man of some learning in language, beyond the modern hatred of Celt priests to the written word."

Artur nodded. "Uther, my father, made certain I was educated in private in the ancient written languages of knowledge of Gaelic and Greek, as well as Latin," said Artur. "Yet I also remember having to attend the ceremonies of the burning of newly discovered manuscripts that the druids demanded. It always struck me as a sign of weakness of these druids that they would be so fearful if men and women could read these ancient texts."

"My lord Artur," said Wulfhere, "The greatest power of any people is education. The manuscript you hold was written by a wise predecessor named Alcuin, who died praying that one day Normen and Celt would unite to rid this land of wilful ignorance."

Ubbe Ragnarsson smiled at Artur. "The first step Artur, is to rebuild schools in the lands of each clan, to that the art of reading and writing may return."

****

Workmen finished the final repairs of a stone building, as young children congregated at its entrance.

****

Lines of men repaired and relayed one side of a road, as a convoy of horse drawn cards and riders negotiated the repaired side of the road.

"We shall repair the roads, so that people may safely travel."

Mercia

****

A hive of activity around a grain storehouse, as carts and people arrived and departed with grain.

"We shall repair and rebuild the storehouses for grain, so that neither vermin, nor man may damage the crop."

****

Pendraig Castle, Pengwern (Shrewsbury)

A sense of life had returned to Pengwern, as a crowd of men and women celebrated with music, brightly coloured banners and a feast outside the castle walls - with the insignia of the red dragon flying high over the battlements.

"Most of all, we shall see life and joy returned to the villages and towns of Mercia and Cambria."

Below, Artur and several kings, including Gyngen of Powys and Osmond of Wicce appeared engaged in animated conversation.

"Surely you must agree Artur," said Osmond of Wicce, "the gods of our ancestors do smile upon us this day!"

Chapter 3

Artur smiled at Osmond of Wicce, as he continued to watch the vibrant celebrations.

"Even moreso Osmond," declared Gyngen of Powys, as he looked at Osmond of Wicce and then Artur, "Artur of Pendraig, is not this feast a sign to end your mourning?"

"Like the sea, no man may control such feelings," replied Artur, "but can only wait with patience until the calm."

An awkward silence, until Artur's sight is captivated by a beautiful young girl (Gwenhwyfawr) dancing traditional Celtic movements with other young maidens. Gyngen of Powys noticed the glance of Artur towards the girl.

"My Lord, you may still be in mourning," he said, "yet your eyes have not lost their sight."

"Who is she?" asked Artur.

"Gwenhwyfawr, daughter of Gwythyr of Gwent. The most beautiful of all the fair young maidens they say in all these lands.

Osmond of Wicce stepped forward alongside Gyngen of Powys and Artur.

"Praise to you Artur for the bounty that we celebrate," said Osmond of Wicce. "But Alas, I fear the snakes of Amorica have awakened."

Artur turned to Osmond of Wicce. "Today we celebrate Osmond. Tomorrow, we may speak of the heavy heart of the business of kings."

"Yes my Lord," replied Osmond of Wicce. "Yet, I have it on good authority and I fear that by tomorrow, the snakes of Æthelred and his brother Ælfred shall have struck at Guyhrum of Daneland and turmoil shall return."

"What harm may two vipers be against the forces of the Danes?" asked Gyngen of Powys dismissively.

Osmond of Wicce shook his head. "Tonight, for respect of our host and this celebration, I shall not bite at your baits Gyngen," smiled Osmond of Wicce. "Only to say that I have received a first hand account that the Amorican merchants purchased for themselves an army of three thousand Moors and that at this very moment have landed in London and Wareham."

Chapter 4

Thames, London

The Thames was crowded with vessels as a flood of Moorish mercenaries fanned out across the city. Only the bodies of dead Danes and rats occupied the streets, while the local population hid as best they could.

Inside the old Roman fort, Æthelred was sitting on the former throne of Guyhrum of Daneland holding onto his crown. Standing in front of him were Æthelweard his chief scribe and the head of the army Æthelwulf.

"My Lord," said Æthelwulf, "the last of the city is secured."

Æthelred nodded as he placed the crown on his head. The crown was too big for his head and it slipped down onto the top of his ears.

"Damn these giant savages," moaned Æthelred.

He threw the crown down onto the stone floor, causing it to bounce across the dead body of Guyhrum of Daneland still strewn on the ground.

"Æthelweard, get me a crown worthy of a king of all the land and beasts," said Æthelred petulantly.

Æthelweard bowed and scampered off as Ælfred entered the room. Ælfred picked up the discarded crown. He paused for a moment and observed the horrified look on the face of Guyhrum of Daneland before moving towards his brother.

"An expensive trophy to so discard my brother," smiled Ælfred, spinning the crown in his fingers.

"Give it back," protested Æthelred. "It is not yours yet Ælfred. In any event, we have just enlarged our plantation by a thousand fold. In one season of trade with our Moor brothers, we will have fully paid for this expedition."

"You might like to make your first proclamation an order to burn the bodies brother," smiled Ælfred. "I don't know about you, but I would rather like to avoid dying of some horrible pox from these rotting Danes."

Ælfred looked at the body of Guyhrum of Daneland and then back at Æthelred.

"Get rid of this," said Æthelred, pointed to the body. "And burn the rest."

The guards nodded obediently and dragged the body away.

"And what about the Normans?" asked Ælfred.

"The bear is still healing its wounds," smiled Æthelred. "Let us not poke it in the eye and attend to the defence of our rightful kingdom."

"And Artur of Pendraig and the Celts of Mercia?" said Ælfred.

"Extend the hand of truce and entreat with them brother," said Æthelred. "If we have them on their word, they shall not harm us, by their own chains of honour."

Ælfred grinned. "Maybe you might last a while as king after all brother."

****

Pendraig Castle, Pengwern (Shrewsbury)

Above the castle of Pengwern, fluttered a giant flag of the red dragon of Pendraig. Inside, Artur and the kings of Powys, Wicce, Ceredig, Glywysing, Gwent and Dyfed were in conference, looking at a map.

"The emissary of Æthelred and the Amoricans, bids us entreat a truce with them," said Bleddri of Dyfed. "That they seek not to extend their gain, but wish to increase their commerce."

"We have gained so much from our truce with Ragnarsson. Our cities be rebuilt, our schools and roads," added Cyngen of Powys. "What more abundance be this possible truce with the Persian merchants?"

"Tell that to the thousands of innocents sold into slavery by these weasels of Wex," growled Gwyon of Ceredig.

"What happened to strike them now, Cyngen of Powys?" asked Bleddri of Dyfed. "Gwyon of Ceredig, you are like the weather!"

"If it is blows you seek, then I shall happily meet you at noon and settle this Bleddri of Dyfed," bellowed Gwyon of Ceredig in reply.

"My Lords. Less haste and let cooler heads prevail," said Artur, trying to calm tempers. "These words of Æthelred and Ælfred certainly be the honeyed music these vipers sung to Guyhrum of Daneland. Yet the law demand that we take a man, especially a king upon his word until he proves himself otherwise unworthy."

Artur pointed to Gwyon of Ceredig. "Gwyon of Ceredig will you be our emissary and counsel, to meet with Æthelred and Ælfred and confirm their terms?" asked Artur.

Chapter 4

"I would prefer to wring the necks of these merchants of flesh, but as you have spoken, I accept this commission," replied Gwyon of Ceredig

"Then go to meet them Gwyon of Ceredig," said Artur, "and until we meet again, may the gods guide and protect you."

Bleddri of Dyfed shook his head negatively. "Artur, these snakes cannot be trusted. For centuries they have been the very essence of evil."

"Then we shall meet them on the neutral ground of Ubbe," smiled Artur. "And woe to the Amoricans if they cannot restrain themselves. For it will be the Norman that make it a holy war for their extinction."

****

London Fort

Æthelred was sitting on a far grander throne, with a magnificent crown in a room now full of colour and movement. Around the room were people dressed in the finest of silks as well as fortune tellers and magicians. Ælfred and his personal bodyguard (Æthelbal) walked into the throne room.

"A handsome crown brother," smiled Ælfred.

"The Celt savages have accepted a meeting for terms of truce, grinned Æthelred. "Go with Æthelwulf and a company of the finest mercenaries and meet them. But refrain from anger or violence, lest you bring doom upon our venture."

"You have nothing to fear brother," grinned Ælfred. "I shall hold my temper against these apes and shall return a hero to our cause."

****

Dorset Village

Ælfred accompanied by Æthelwulf and Æthelbal and a cadre of Moorish mercenaries ride along a road entering a village.

"My Lord, the meeting is upon the neutral territory of Cambria at Dorset," said Æthelwulf.

Ælfred slowed down as he noticed some young children playing next to a stone wall. They stopped and look at the strangers as they enter the village.

"What fine children these be!" exclaimed Ælfred,

"They be under the protection of Ragnarsson my Lord," said Æthelwulf.

Chapter 4

Ælfred reached into a bag at the back of his saddle and produced some sweets and lent down to some of the children, who came over to look.

"Sweets, children?" Ælfred asked softly.

"My lord," said Æthelwulf nervously.

"What harm be there Æthelwulf to pick a few apples before one becomes the owner of the orchard?" smiled Ælfred.

From a house nearby, two women appeared from a side door and spot the children as they eat the sweets of Ælfred. They rushed forward and quickly scooped up the boys, dragging them inside the house, shutting the door. As the children were hurried away, Ælfred became enraged.

"Seize them Æthelwulf!" yelled Ælfred. "Seize all of them, that we may return to London with at least some token for this damned excursion."

Æthelwulf nodded and signalled to the guards. They alighted from their horses and moved to the house, bashing the door down. A few moments later the sound of screams and then silence as the young terrified boys were dragged out to Ælfred.

At that very moment Gwyon of Ceredig and his troop approached from the other direction and spot the commotion.

"This be sacred and neutral ground Amorican, as your brother Æthelred requested," yelled Gwyon of Ceredig. "It be under the protection of Ragnarsson."

"You speak savage," said Ælfred condescendingly. "But I recognize not your authority."

"And you bring a whole troop when since the earliest of times, such terms was always with but an agent," protested Gwyon of Ceredig.

"Old rules are for the dead," sneered Ælfred. "I am the law, therefore the law is whatever I say it is for my people."

"Alas, I come from Artur of Pendraig and all our clans in honour and good faith, to find nothing but a fox in a hen house," replied Gwyon of Ceredig, as he drew his sword in defence.

"Then, I shall return the message to Artur and your brethren," growled Ælfred as Æthelwulf and the troop of soldiers surrounded Gwyon of Ceredig and his attendants.

"Seize them!" screamed Ælfred.

Before Gwyon of Ceredig or any of his personal guard could manoeuvre, the mercenaries of Ælfred seized the Celts and kill all except for Gwyon of Ceredig. They drag him before Ælfred.

Chapter 4

Ælfred got off his horse and walked over to Gwyon of Ceredig sprawled on the ground at the point of several swords.

"Do you know nothing of the honour of your word and that of your brother?" said Gwyon of Ceredig defiantly.

"Your stubborn adherence to ancient notions will be your doom," grinned Ælfred. "Commerce is war. Promises are made to be broken and history will prove our kind as victors."

At that moment, Ælfred thrust his sword into the chest of Gwyon of Ceredig.

"Curse you and your kind," yelled Gwyon of Ceredig with his last breath.

"Too late. Your gods already did."

Ælfred stabbed him again and Gwyon of Ceredig was dead.

****

London

Ælfred entered the throne room, to find it devoid of all life and merriment, except for the solemn figure of his brother Æthelred, sitting on the throne.

Mercia

Before Ælfred had even taken a dozen steps toward his brother, Æthelred jumped up and launched himself at Ælfred, slapping him hard across the face.

"You idiot," screamed Æthelred hysterically. "You have killed us."

"Steady brother," replied Ælfred, nursing his cheek. "We sent a message remember?"

"It is not the undisciplined Celts I fear, but the might of the Normans upon our necks," replied Æthelred.

"A war for a few pretty children?" said Ælfred looking perplexed.

"It makes no difference if it had been one cow," said Æthelred shaking his head negatively. "You took what was not yours. You fool! Now the Normans must attack or face civil upheaval."

Ælfred shrugged his shoulders. "Then blame yourself for putting your merchant brother in such conflict," he mumbled petulantly.

Chapter 5

Pendraig Castle, Pengwern (Shrewsbury)

Artur sat with his head in his hands as Osmond of Wicce and Gwythyr of Gwent were in counsel with him.

"You are not responsible for the evil in men's hearts, nor their deeds," said Gwythyr of Gwent.

"Yet a brave king and his men were lost on my insistence of honour," said Artur in reply.

"And more may yet follow my lord Artur," said Osmond of Wicce. "For what be a man, if he stands for nothing?"

At that moment the doors burst open with Owell of Glywysing barreling into the room.

"Kill them," growled Owell of Glywysing. "Kill all these rats."

"Yet they dishonoured their neutrality with Ubbe Ragnarsson as the deed was upon his land," said Artur.

"Our land," added Owell of Glywysing.

"Is that what you want Owell of Glywysing?" asked Artur. "That the Amorican merchants once again succeed in divining and conquering so that like vultures they may profit from their unholy trade of war for commerce? For I fear all will be dust if clearer heads do not prevail."

"What then is your plan?" asked Osmond of Wicce

"I shall ride to Lindor and seek counsel with Ubbe," said Artur. "I sense he too is anxious not to allow the weasels of Wex to break the truce between us."

****

Lindor (Lincoln) Castle, Cambria

Ubbe Ragnarsson and Ivar Olik in full battle dress, were studying a map along with two of his generals Arni Erlingr and Oddr Sigurdr, when a Norman guard (Porir) rushed over.

"My lords," said the guard named Porir. "King Artur of Pendraig is here and seeks urgent audience."

The men stopped speaking and look up as Artur entered.

"My Lord Ubbe," said Artur bowing as Ubbe and his council repeat the honour to Artur.

"Artur, these merchants of death have slain a good king," said Ubbe Ragnarsson. "Yet they have also breached the sacred bond of our people. Thus, as the protector of the people, it is my solemn duty to punish them and destroy such evil."

"We are both dishonoured," said Artur.

"I fear the peace between our people may be tested beyond its limit if some see us ride together Artur of Pendraig," replied Ubbe Ragnarsson. "There are more snakes yet to be seen. Better you continue to keep the peace and let my army deal with this menace."

Artur and Ubbe embrace by clasping of the arm to the elbow.

"May Heaven and the Ancestors protect you," smiled Artur. "Godspeed."

****

Lindon Outskirts

The Norman army was on the move from Lindor. An endless line of cavalry, bowmen and lancers marched with purpose toward inevitable conflict.

****

London

Æthelred, dressed in elaborate armour along with Ælfred were looking at maps with Æthelwulf. Nearby several clearly Moorish officers, also observe the planning.

"The Normans are on the move and will reach London in three days," said Æthelwulf. "But Ragnarsson will want to rest his troops for a day before any attack, so if we advance out of London, we may catch his army before they have had time to recuperate."

"Why not stay in London and defend the city?" asked Æthelred

"Because my Lord we have neither the defences, nor the provisions nor the will of the people to sustain any siege for more than a few days," said Æthelwulf in reply.

"Why not ransom the people or use them as our shields?" added Ælfred. "Surely we could appeal to that thing they call honour?"

Æthelwulf shook his head.

"My Lord, there is no other way," said Æthelwulf, ignoring Ælfred and stared straight at Æthelred. "You must lead us into battle."

"Why me?" protested Æthelred. "You are the head of the army."

Chapter 5

"Because my Lord, it is the expected duty of the king to lead his men into battle, as it has always been done," replied Æthelwulf dryly.

"Why all these stupid rules about what a king is supposed to do?" moaned Æthelred, stomping his feet in protest. "What if he does not? What then?"

"Then I fear, you would be better killing yourselves now as even mercenaries are men first," said Æthelwulf.

A heavy silence before Æthelred shrugged his shoulders in resignation. "Cease tormenting us general," he grumbled, "and pray tell us where you wish me to place my life in your hands?"

Æthelwulf pointed to a position on the map which reads as Reading.

"Here my Lords. At Reading."

Æthelred looked over at his brother.

"Then Ælfred you wait for the new mercenaries to arrive from Spain and make haste to this place," added Æthelred, "as Æthelwulf and I come separately. While we engage, it will be up to you Ælfred to outflank the monster and kill it."

****

Mercia

Reading, Wessex Lines

Æthelred and Æthelwulf stand at the top of a hill as they watch the mass of Normans arrive opposite and begin arranging themselves for battle.

"There are so many of them general," said Æthelred nervously.

"Only about a thousand or so my Lord," replied Æthelwulf. "Yet you have forty five hundred."

"Is that enough?" exclaimed Æthelred. "They are so big. Maybe we should wait for Ælfred and the reinforcements?"

"You are the commander of this battle, my Lord."

****

Reading, Norman Lines

Ragnarsson and his generals Ivar Olik, Oddr Sigurdr and Arni Erlinger surveyed the lines of the Moor mercenaries.

"A mercenary army. A forest of reeds," said Ubbe Ragnarsson. "Upon one swift blow and mighty wind, they shall buckle and fold. For no man but a lunatic sacrifices his life just for blood money."

Ubbe signalled to Oddr Sigurdr.

Chapter 5

"Send word to the men. Let them scream as loud as tormented spirits and bang their shields," he smiled. "Let us see the metal in their swords."

Oddr bowed and moved away. In the background the sound of barking orders and the thud of footsteps in unison and clashing metal as the Normans begin their advance towards the mercenaries of Æthelred.

****

Reading, Wessex Lines

Æthelwulf rode forward and looked out toward the Normans as the Normans continue to advance at a faster and faster pace.

"They shall soon charge at our lines, my lord. What is your command?" asked Æthelwulf.

Æthelred did not respond.

"My Lord," said Æthelwulf insistently.

"I do not know," mumbled Æthelred. "What would you suggest is best we do?"

"It is too late for that my Lord," said Æthelwulf in reply.

"I am but a businessman. I am but a merchant," said Æthelred nervously. "You are the general. You lead."

With that, Æthelred turned and rode away, followed by his body guards, leaving Æthelwulf and the mercenary generals behind. Many of the mercenaries in the lines see Æthelred ride away.

"Then I shall see you soon on the other side merchant," shouted Æthelwulf, before trying to calm the ranks of mercenaries. "Hold the line!" yelled Æthelwulf. "Hold the line!"

****

Reading Battle Lines

Ubbe Ragnarsson and his cavalry advanced to the centre of the Moor mercenary lines and then split off to the side, while the Norman lance men ran toward the mercenary lines, screaming and bashing their shields like a roaring storm.

Within but a few feet and before even the first blows were cast by the Normans, the lines of mercenaries buckled as hundreds of mercenaries began to flee, even before a single Norman had struck a blow.

Once the Normans reached the mercenary lines, they cut through without losing any momentum.

Chapter 5

Within an instant, the whole mercenary army collapsed into retreat.

****

Upon the scene of the carnage of the retreating mercenary army, Ælfred arrived with his military counsel Ætheling. He watched stunned as the Normans obliterated the Moor mercenaries.

"My Lord. My Lord," said Ætheling to Ælfred. "It is too late. We have lost the field. Fall back and regroup."

Ætheling nodded and signalled for the men to withdraw.

Mercia

Chapter 6

Reading, Battle Field

Ubbe Ragnarsson finished off the life of another mercenary, before he paused to survey the utter slaughter. In the space of less than half an hour, the Normans had killed twice their number and sent the surviving mercenaries fleeing. Ivar Olik was standing nearby and signalled to Ubbe to look beyond at the forces of Ælfred withdrawing, without engaging.

"One coward at a time Ivar, yelled Ubbe. "First, find Æthelred. Then we shall deal with Ælfred."

****

Stonehenge

Ubbe Ragnarsson, Ivar Olik and a troop of cavalry rode up in front of the ancient and largely intact Stonehenge monument. A group of Normans surrounded some prisoners kneeling on the ground. One of the prisoners was Æthelred. Ubbe Ragnarsson stepped down off his horse and moved over.

As soon as Æthelred saw Ubbe, he fell to the ground, holding out his hands.

"Have mercy Ubbe Ragnarsson."

"And what does an Amorican merchant, know of virtue or mercy?" asked Ubbe, unsheathing his sword and moving to the position of Æthelred sprawled on the ground.

"My house will pay you a handsome reward of gold if you spare my life?"

"That is better," grinned Ubbe. "Now you reveal your true colours. For I swore upon the dying breath of my father to be a just king. But I can kill a rat with a clear conscience. Get up!"

Æthelred shook his head negatively and instead started sobbing, on the ground.

"Get up and at least die like a man," growled Ubbe as two Norman guard moved over to grab Æthelred. But before they could grab his arms, Ubbe Ragnarsson thrust his sword into the chest of Æthelred.

"Very well, die like the parasite you are, if that is your choice," growled Ubbe, as Æthelred screamed then fell dead.

Ubbe Ragnarsson wiped the tip of his sword on nearby grass, before sheathing it.

Chapter 6

"Still you were a man and so I shall pray for your soul," he said, before turning to get back on his horse.

Ivor Olik approached Ubbe on horseback.

"Our riders have spotted the forces of Ælfred at Salisbury," said Ivor.

"They are doubling back towards London," replied Ubbe. "Send word and move the main forces to cut them off. We shall run them like rabbits into the jaws of our men."

"My Lord, I urge caution," said Ivor. "Even if they reach London, we can defeat them."

"Ivor, let this be the end," added Ubbe. "Though it may be to my regret, I have become weary at chasing these demons and shadows."

Ivor nodded as the forces split off with Ubbe Ragnarsson to depart in one direction while Ubbe, Ivor Olik and the others ride off in a different direction.

****

Salisbury Plain

Ælfred and Ætheling were sitting on their horses with other cavalry as a messenger approached hard toward them. He stopped and bowed.

Mercia

"My Lord your brother is dead," said the messenger. "At the sacred stones of Amesbury not far from here."

The messenger handed the crown of Æthelred to Ælfred who put it upon his head.

"What be your orders, my Lord?" asked Ætheling.

Ælfred took off the crown and then his outer coat and then handed them to Ætheling.

"I pray Ætheling you let us effect an escape, replied Ælfred. For if the monster Normans see you as I, then I may be able to obtain an advantage."

"By what direction do you seek?" asked Ætheling.

"Ætheling if you and the main forces ride West towards Exeter, we shall seek refuge at Winchester as common travellers before breaking to London," said Ælfred. "There I shall send for ships to aid in your escape or reinforcements."

Ætheling placed the crown upon his head and put the cloak upon himself.

"As you command my Lord," said Ætheling in reply.

"Ætheling do not lose that which is mine," added Ælfred. "Soon I will call upon it again upon my head at London."

Chapter 6

Ætheling and the primary forces departed, leaving Ælfred accompanied by only his personal bodyguard Æthelbal.

Mercia

Chapter 7

Winchester

Ælfred and Æthelbal hidden as travellers, rode into the city of Winchester, toward a thick stonewall building, the Hyde Abbey.

They got off their horses and approached the door to the Abbey.

"My Lord, best conceal all weaponry," said Æthelbal. "For the abbot shall refuse such entry to any man who is armed."

Æthelbal looked around and saw a ruined stone field wall opposite. Ælfred handed him his sword and Æthelbal concealed their weapons behind the stone field wall before knocking on the abbey door.

The door opened to reveal Abbot Runi Emery.

"How may I help you men?" the Abbot asked politely.

"Abbot, we be peaceful and unarmed Christian travellers on our way to London," replied Æthelbal. "We pray our delay has left us without safe lodging. May we enter? For we be willing to make a donation?"

"All men of god who come in peace are welcome," smiled the Abbott. "Come, please enter."

The door was opened and Ælfred and Æthelbal walked their horses through the door as it is closed behind them.

Inside, the Abbot escorted Ælfred and Æthelbal through the main hall.

"Unfortunately you men have missed the evening meal," said the Abbott. "But you are welcome to freshen up and join us for vespers after which I am sure we can offer you a little sustenance."

"Thank you. It has been a long journey," smiled Æthelba. "I fear our singing may not add to your prayers. We shall adjourn for our own silent prayer by your leave."

The abbot nodded and continued to escort the men through the hall.

****

Winchester

Ubbe Ragnarsson, Oddr Sigurdr and a small troop of men entered Winchester.

Chapter 7

Ubbe Ragnarsson, Oddr Sigurdr and the men stop out the front of the Hyde Abbey, alighting from their horses. Ubbe Ragnarsson took off his sword and armour, handing them to Oddr Sigurdr.

"These are Christian men of honour and neither sword, nor the stain of the blood of another man be permitted to enter here without curse," said Ubbe.

"My Lord," replied Oddr Sigurdr.

"Let me first call upon the Abbot and then I shall pray and rest," said Ubbe. "Stay alert and I shall see you in the morn."

The men nod as Ragnarsson banged upon the door. Soon after the Abbot came and opened the door, immediately recognising Ubbe Ragnarsson.

"My Lord," said the Abbott. "An unexpected honour at this late hour."

"Be there room for some old bones?" smiled Ubbe.

The abbot smiled and embraced Ubbe.

"No Soldier of Christ shall ever be denied sanctuary from the evils of this world," replied the Abbot.

Ubbe entered with the Abbot and the door closes. Inside, the Abbot escorted Ubbe Ragnarsson along the Cloister past the cells of the monks.

Ælfred and Æthelbal are in the same cell, with the door slightly closed whispering a conversation when they hear the Abbot and Ubbe Ragnarsson in conversation walking past. Æthelbal puts his finger to his lips to tell Ælfred to be quiet.

The Abbot and Ubbe Ragnarsson stopped at a cell, a few doors down from the cell in which Æthelbal and Ælfred are intently hearing the conversation outside.

"Pray for the soul of Æthelred and all the men who died today Abbot," said Ubbe.

"The Divine Commission of one who fights against evil is a heavy burden my Lord," replied the Abbott. "Evil must be rooted out wherever it is found, lest it be allowed to thrive. The weasels of Wex have raped this land for too long. Bless you Ubbe."

Ubbe nodded and turns into his cell, closing the door.

Ælfred and Æthelbal wait until the Abbot has passed before even making a sound.

"It is Ubbe Ragnarsson my Lord," whispered Æthelbal.

"But why would he shelter here unarmed?" asked Ælfred.

"Because he is a man of faith," whispered Æthelbal in reply.

Ælfred smiled.

Chapter 7

****

Ubbe Ragnarsson knelt in prayer on the stone floor in front of a bed as the door opened. He didn't turn around.

"Thank you," Ubbe said quietly. "But I seek no sustenance."

The sound of the door closing and then a knife held at the throat of Ubbe Ragnarsson by Æthelbal with Ælfred next to him.

"How does one kill a rat that hides within the sacred sanctuary of the Divine, without damaging that which is most sacred?" said Ubbe.

"The man who is prepared to even deceive the gods is the only one that can assure survival," replied Ælfred.

"Do your worst," replied Ubbe. "For one day merchant, your kind shall be held to account."

"Maybe. I doubt it. But certainly not today."

Both Æthelbal and Ælfred thrust their knives into the body of Ubbe Ragnarsson and he fell to the ground mortally wounded.

****

Mercia

Hyde Abbey, Winchester

Oddr Sigurdr and the men outside the Abbey were half asleep before being woken by the strange glow from the windows of the Abbey that changed to shades of orange as smoke began to billow from all exits.

The doors to the Abbey swung open and monks began pouring out as flames started lashing from within the structure. The Normans pushed past the escaping monks and rush toward the entrance. But the intensity of the heat and flames pushed them back.

Chapter 8

Pengwern

The flying flag of the red dragon of Pendraig atop the castle of Pengwern. Inside Artur was in meeting with Gwythyr of Gwent when a messenger arrived.

"My Lord," spoke the messenger. "Ubbe has fallen to the treachery of Ælfred who breached the most sacred honour of Sanctuary in order to execute his filthy deed."

Artur bowed his head. "Then a great light for peace has been snuffed out."

"Yes, but Artur, your bonds of obligation are also broken," said Gwythyr of Gwent.

"Be that it may," replied Artur, "I shall go to Lindor to respect the memory of Ubbe."

"I caution you Artur. For halfdane be not like his brother and is short of temper and fond of cruelty."

"Then we shall be in the hands of the gods Gwythyr," smiled Artur.

****

Lindor

A long funeral procession led by Halfdane, followed the body of Ubbe Ragnarson. Artur was one of the dignitaries walking immediately behind. The procession passed through the gates of Lincoln down to the river. There, the body of Ubbe was loaded onto a boat, before oarsmen cast off and the boat travelled away downstream toward the sea.

****

Lindor Castle, Hall

Halfdane was sitting on the former throne of his brother, surrounded by guards and his head bodyguard (Brandr Asmundr) as Artur approached.

"My brother trusted you and treated you as if an equal," said Halfdane.

"I mourn for the loss of your brother," replied Artur. "As do all our people."

"As is the law, his estate now falls to my inheritance that I be now king of all Northcambria and Cambria," said Halfdane. "Pledge now your fealty unto me Artur, that you serve me as you served my brother."

"An ally and friend of your brother we be, not servants or slaves," added Artur.

"You dare challenge my word Pendraig?" growled Halfdane. "I warn you as I be less forgiving than my half brother."

"As your brother himself forewarned me is true," smiled Artur. "Yet I came under truce to grieve for your brother, not to speak terms for which I have no counsel."

"Then you shall wait hear as my guest, until you are ready or such other counsel come," said Halfdane, signalling to Brandr Asmundr next to him, who with several other Norman guards surrounded Artur and lead him away.

Artur was led down by the guards to the terrible dungeons of Lindor Castle. They shuffled past the harrowing images of tortured and emaciated men.

The Norman guards put him in chains and threw into a dark cell, with the door slamming closed behind him.

****

Mercia

Holly Head Castle

The kings Cyngen of Powys, Osmond of Wicce, Owell of Glywysing, Gwythyr of Gwent and Bleddri of Dyfed rode to the gates of Holly Head Castle.

Gwynedd and several guards came out and stopped them at the gates.

"Halt. State your purpose," demanded Gwynedd.

"Gwynedd, son of Rhodri. Cease acting as a troll and take these kings to your father."

Gwynedd huffed and signalled for the gates of Holly Head Castle to be lifted. Soon after, the men rode in.

Inside the castle, Rhodri of the Angels was sitting upon a great throne reading a manuscript with a magnifying glass as the kings presented themselves.

"Alas the fate of mice and men," smiled Rhodri of the Angels. "Did I not warn thee of the folly embracing the cup of the beasts?"

"Spare us the epilogue Rhodri," responded Gwythyr of Gwent. "Where do you stand?"

"Where I always have Gwythyr of Gwent. As a servant to the Holly and a defender of the sacred truth of Tara. What say you?"

Chapter 8

"I too still honour our ancient virtues," replied Gwythyr of Gwent, "but value first the hard won peace of our people."

"But at what cost?" asked Rhodri of the Angels. "I did not doubt the genuine cause of Artur. Maybe he now be dead in the clutches of the Halfdane? Maybe not. But what price be this peace you speak so passionately?"

Bleddri of Dyfed stepped forward. "For too many generations Rhodri, our people died fighting one another over such petty squabbles that we deserved nothing more than to be known as savages," he said. "Now in one generation our children are at learning, our roads repaired, our fields restored. Is this not worth fighting for?"

"And if you manage to defeat the Norman of Halfdane, what next?" asked Rhodri of the Angels. "I too have heard that the godless Ælfred of the Amorican slave traders is still at large. How many more monsters still to slay?"

"So the great Rhodri of the Holly Angels, chooses to do nothing to stand against the face of tyranny," said Osmond of Wicce.

"Do not test my hospitality Osmond of Wicce," growled Rhodri of the Angels, "lest I forget my ancestry."

"Then act," said Cyngen of Powys. "If not for Artur, then for the cause of our faith. Better we die in honour against evil, than live under the yoke of fear."

****

Lindor Castle, Dungeons

The door to the dungeon cell opened revealing the shivering and dirty figure of Artur, crawled up in a ball. Ivor Olik entered with a plate of food, a pitcher and a blanket.

"Forgive us Lord," said Ivor. "Halfdane does not speak for all Norman."

Artur looked up as the plate of food was handed to him and he grabbed it, devouring the bread and cheese. Ivor placed a blanket over him.

"Halfdane has his men everywhere and so it was not safe until now to visit."

Artur gulped from the pitcher then adjusted the blanket around himself, while still eating.

Chapter 8

"I have no quarrel with any man, but the ideas that drive them," replied Artur. "Thank you for your kindness."

Ivor turned back to the prison door.

Mercia

Chapter 9

Lindor Castle, Hall

Halfdane was sitting on the throne, signing papers, with Brandr Asmundr and Ivor Olik by his side as Artur was brought before him in chains and rags.

"I do not believe in torture Artur," said Halfdane without looking up. "I believe the mind of a man, be his worst enemy. Gently deprive him of all that makes him a man and even the strongest will yield in hunger for the slop of pigs."

"If it is consent you seek, then I have none to give," replied Artur.

"Indeed, consent before the Divine without duress," smiled Halfdane finally looking at Artur directly. "A delicate dance. Therefore, I be a patient man."

At the end of the main hall, a Norman Guard (Njall) rushed frantically into the hall along with several other guards.

"My Lord," said Njall, bowing his head and still trying to catch his breath.

Halfdane looked at him sternly.

"My Lord," continued Njall, "the Celts have amassed outside the gates of the city."

"It seems your tribe has not abandoned you after all Artur," grinned Halfdane as he got up from his throne and signalled for the guards to pick up Artur and follow him.

Halfdane then walked through the corridors to the ramparts of the castle and looked out at the horizon.

"How many do you estimate?" asked Halfdane to Norman Guard Njall

"All of them, my Lord."

****

Lindor Outskirts

A mass of men on foot and in full armour, stretching for as far as the eye could see. Behind them were men on horseback and at the centre, countless flags.

Observing the scene was Rhodri Mawr, accompanied by his son Gwynedd and the Kings of Cyngen of Powys, Osmond of Wicce, Owell of Glywysing, Gwythyr of Gwent and Bleddri of Dyfed.

"This will be bloody my Lords," said Rhodri of Angels to the other kings.

"Not a bad day to die," smiled Gwythyr of Gwent

Chapter 9

"Lets have some music then shall we?" replied Rhodri of Angels.

Rhodri Mawr looked over at an officer nearby.

"Bring forth the pipers and drums," he commanded.

The officer nodded, turned his horse and moved forward to the lines.

"Pipes and Drums!" he yelled at the top of his lungs, and the order was echoed down the line.

Like the waking drone of a giant machine, the warming tones of the pipes as they come into life, in time with the definitive rolling thunder of hundreds of drums in union.

Soon the air was bursting with the unmistakable sound of hundreds of bag pipes playing in unison with the drums as both the pipers and drummers move forward of the ground troops.

******

Lindor Castle, Battlements

Halfdane looked out at the sight of the largest united Celtic army he has ever seen. Next to him was Artur, in chains and rags, smiling and looking slightly taller. Ivor Olik, Brandr Asmundr and the guards stood behind them.

"As we see," said Halfdane, "few things unite the Celts except injustice."

Halfdane signalled to Brandr Asmundr. "Take Artur back to his cell," he said. "If the Celts breach the walls, kill him."

Brandr nodded and Artur was led away with chains. Halfdane then turned to Ivor.

"Ivor prepare the defences. Every man who can walk must fight. And those not prepared to fight, kill them immediately."

"As you order my Lord," replied Ivor. "I fear not an honourable death. But should we not consider the possibility of terms, lest there be the slaughter of so many thousands of women and children?"

"Ivor, we lost more than half our people gaining these lands when the Celts were divided. God help us if they become united. Let then this be a defining moment to break their spirit once and for all."

Ivor nodded and moved away.

****

Lindor Castle, Hallway

Chapter 9

In the middle of a major passageway, Ivor Olik, Oddr Sigurdr and Arni Erlinger stand in conversation, as men rush past them to their positions.

"Arni, hold fire to the last possible moment," said Ivor to Arni Erlinger, before looking at Oddr Sigurdr. "Oddr, make sure your men are in place instead of Halfdane's men and when the Celts are within range, open the gates. I will deal with Halfdane."

Arni and Oddr both nod affirmatively.

"For the memory of Ubbe and for the lives of our children, let us pray we survive this madness," said Ivor Olik and the men disburse.

****

Lindor Outskirts

Rhodri and the kings watch as their forces move closer to the walls of the city, yet without being fired upon.

"What strange game this be of Halfdane?" commented Rhodri of Angels. "Our men are in range, yet they do not fire?"

"Perhaps my Lord, there is more intrigue in the Norman court than meets the eye?" suggested Osmond of Wicce.

Soon after the gates to the city open and upon this sign, the Celt forces race toward the entrances.

"They are surrendering!" exclaimed Bleddri of Dyfed.

"The men of Ubbe possibly. But caution to the presumption of the men of the Halfdane yet conceding," added Gwythyr of Gwent.

Chapter 10

Lindor Castle, Dungeons

The door to the dungeon cell swung open and Ivor Olik entered carrying clean garments, boots and a cloak.

He immediately moved over to Artur and started to unshackle him. "Put these on," he said. "We have little time."

Artur was startled at first, feeling the weight lifted from his wrists, before he began to get dressed.

"Halfdane is determined to damn us all," he whispered.

At that moment, Brandr Asmundr entered the cell and thrust his sword at Artur and Ivor Olik stepped in front to catch the force of the

"Damn you traitor," yelled Brandr Asmundr.

Yet before Brandr could thrust his sword again, Ivor swivelled around in agony and thrust a shorter blade into the neck of Brandr who fell back profusely bleeding and collapsed onto the ground dead.

Ivor slumped down as Artur grabbed him and struggled to bring him to his feet.

"You are deeply wounded my friend," said Artur to Ivor, as Artur picked up the sword of Brandr Asmundr.

"It is nothing. I still have some life. We must leave now, we remain yet in gravest peril my Lord," replied Ivor, steadying himself.

Artur helped Ivor out of the cell only to be confronted by Halfdane and three other Normans.

"A traitor and his master caught in our midst," growled Halfdane. "Very well. I may not survive this day, but you two will certainly not."

Halfdane lunged at Artur, who was still unsteady on his feet with a sword. Ivor stepped forward and checked the advance of Halfdane, shoving him back against the other men.

Two of the soldiers manoeuvred around to try and attack Ivor from the other side, forcing him to engage them, as Halfdane and one of the Norman guards attack at Artur, who defended himself.

"Your stay has weakened you I see Artur," grinned Halfdane. "No longer the great warrior."

"There is still enough in me Halfdane, to despatch one more tyrant," replied Artur.

Ivor, while gravely wounded still despatched the two soldiers. But before he could engage the other, Halfdane swivelled around and thrust his sword into his chest.

Chapter 10

Ivor collapsed to the ground mortally wounded. But in the same instant, Artur managed to kill the third Norman guard. Halfdane turned around and caught the side of the blade of the sword of Artur, pulling it out of his grip.

"Farewell, thee Artur."

But before Halfdane could land his blow, Ivor in one final burst upon his knees, thrust his sword through the chest of Halfdane and out the other side. Ivor collapsed to the ground.

Artur rushed over to him.

"Ivor, you saved my life not once but twice. I promise I shall protect your children and all the Norman people as my own."

Ivor smiled.

"My Lord...There is a heavy burden I must release before I die... Ubbe made me avow..Your son..Your son.."

Ivor closes his eyes.

"What is it Ivor?"

Ivor died. Artur got up and hurried to the stairs leading from the dungeon.

******

Mercia

Lindor City Gates

Rhodri and the kings rode at the head of their cavalry. They entered the city to the applause of the people and the protection of their soldiers lining the path, as they approached the battlements of the castle proper.

****

Lindor Castle, Hallway

Artur moved along the hallway of Lindor castle as Norman fought Norman, the men of Halfdane being slain.

****

Lindor Castle, Battlements

Upon the Battlements of the castle, a lone archer sneaked up on the sight below. Carefully, he took aim at Rhodri Mawr and fired. The arrow struck Rodri Mawr in the chest and he fell off his horse, causing immediate panic.

Chapter 10

At that moment, Artur reached the battlements of the Castle and seized the archer, throwing him off and screaming down onto the ground below. The Celts looked up and see Artur, hold his sword up. A loud roar erupted, as Gwynedd and others attended to Rhodri.

****

Lindor Castle, Royal Chambers

Upon the former bed of Ubbe and Halfdane, Rhodri now lay, mortally wounded. Surrounding him were the kings, including Artur. Rhodri momentarily regained consciousness, opening his eyes. He looked at Artur.

"This be the prize for which I gave my life?"

Muffled laughter from the Kings.

"My Lord, the arrow be too close to the heart."

"Befitting then Artur, that I die of the malady that all men suffer if they truly love this land."

Rhodri reached out and held the hand of Artur.

"Be the wise king we need. Do not let foolish old men, distract you from the truth of restoring one law for all men in liberty, fraternity and virtue."

Artur nodded as Gwynedd came forward.

"I could not be more proud of you my son."

Rhodri signalled to Gwynedd.
"Now son do what he commands."
With that Rhodri closed his eyes and died.

****

Holly Head Fields

Artur, Gwynedd, his brother (Anarawd) and the united
kings stood around the grave of Rhodri Mawr as he
was interred in a stone mausoleum. Gwynedd stepped
forward.

"Upon the death of our father the great Holly King
of the Angels," he said, "we pledge ourselves to unite
under one rule of law for all, governed by the belief
that all men possess rights of liberty and fraternity
through virtue. Therefore, upon this day and with your
help we pledge our union with the great kingdom of
Mercia."

Chapter 11

Midst an ancient forest, a vast new clearing had been made. A space now full of thousands of people, horses, tents and flags.

At the centre of the gathering stood a huge untouched Holly tree. Around the tree was assembled a gathering of kings and nobles from the furthest corners of the island of Britain.

Artur was standing in this great circle of kings surrounded by a sea of flags. Many faces were familiar such as Osmond of Wicce, Owell of Glywysing, Gwythyr of Gwent, Bleddri of Dyfed, Cyngen of Powys and Gwynedd of Angels.

Some however, were new to such unity as were Ceowulf Of Cent, Oswald Of Dommoc, Aelle Of Weald, Atwal Of Sealwud, Sigered Of Mid Angles, Masgwid Of Elmet and Constantine Of Alba.

Myrddin Of Dumnonia stood out above all others in, dressed in pure white, with the Christian cross and sun upon his vestments, complete with gold mitre. Artur stepped forward from the kings.

"My Lords, my kings," he said, "may the memory of this day echo in the hearts and minds of all here present and those yet to come. Truly, never has there been a greater assembly upon these lands and sacred isle."

Artur moved forward and greeted each of the kings in the circle, clasping each of their hands to the elbow, saying:

"To the north, we honour Holly King Constantine of Alba and King Masgwid of Elmet. To the West we honour King Gwynedd of Angels, King Cyngen of Powys, King Bleddri of Dyfed, King Owell of Glywysing and King Gwythyr of Gwent. To the mid we honour King Osmond of Wicce and King Sigered of Mide Angles. To the east we honour King Oswald of Dommoc and King Ceolwulf of Cent. To the south we honour King Aelle of Weald and King Atwal of Sealwud. To the south west we honour the great Bisheop King Myrddin of Dumnonia."

Artur returned to the centre of the circle.

"North, West, East, South and Centre. Scarcely has there been a moment of peace among the people on these lands for countless generations. The Phoenicians, the Romans, the Persians who called themselves Amoricans, the Danes and the Normans. All have come to these shores. Yet when we have not been fighting such invaders for our survival, we have been resigned to warring amongst ourselves. Some of these invaders exploited, for their own advantage, our shortness of temper and quickness to judgement. Others showed us the folly of our ways, in that if we remain divided, none shall survive."

Artur flicked some leaves from the ground into the air and let them slowly fall to earth.

"What shall we do? Before we can unite, we must learn to trust again. And to trust, we need a place, a most sacred place to call a sanctuary. A place where there be no arms, no difference between Christian and Celt; no difference between one tribe or another. A place where no truce need be called, for such sacred place above all others be guarded by Heaven. This shall be that place. Here, at the sacred centre of our Island, within the ancient forest of Ardu, around the great Holly Tree, we form a new oath and a new covenant at this place we shall call Coventry."

There was a roar from the crowd and from the kings.

"Around its branches, we shall build a sanctuary for all Kings and a union of all united kingdoms. Let no man now or forever more, defile this most holy of holy places, lest they be judged by heaven. For here at Coventry be the first place and the first time we unite as one people, under one union and rule of law in honour and dignity."

The crowd roared again.

****

Coventry Clearing, Ardu Forest

Great fires were burning as music was playing and people were drinking and singing. Artur was speaking with King Constantine of Alba, as Myrddin of Dumnonia stepped closer.

"I respect your sense at calming the Normans with their own lands and leaders Artur," said Constantine, "but feeding the wolf only defers, not defeats destiny."

Constantine looked over to the side at Oddr Sigurdr who was now the bodyguard of Artur, as Myrddin entered the conversation.

"Fine speech young Artur," smiled Myrddin. "You would have made a great emperor in different times."

"The Great King Myrddin of Dumnonia," added Constantine.

Myrddin waved his hand.

"A mere servant to our collective cause Constantine of Alba. Nothing more."

"Lord Myrddin I am honoured you chose to attend," replied Artur.

"I may be stubborn Artur," said Myrddin, "but I am not so stupid as to throw away my witness to history."

Myrddin signalled to Constantine.

"Excuse me Constantine, may I have a brief word with Artur in privy?"

Constantine nodded and departed their company. Artur and Myrddin found themselves in a brief moment of privacy midst the celebrations all around them.

"Artur you have achieved such things, that not even I, a man accustomed to foresight dreamt possible. Yet, I fear such goodwill can easily be lost, if not clear and decisive governance be considered."

"My Lord, your fame as a teacher and master of all wisdom will be known for eternity. Yet, I am no scholar."

"And this is the problem Artur. The Amoricans hire dozens of scribes, both for their accounting and to write obscene lies to pass off as history. Ælfred has commissioned two of the brightest in Nennius and Asser to write a wholly absurd new fable of epic proportions. All the while, the Celts remain illiterate to their own story and law."

"Yet I helped repair the academies in many centres Myrddin."

"It is not enough Artur."

At that moment, Osmond of Wicce and Cyngen of Powys approached and interrupted the conversation.

"My Lords. Lord Myrddin. Tis a night of celebration, not melancholy."

Myrddin of Dumnonia bowed to Osmond of Wicce. "You are correct Osmond of Wicce," smiled Myrddin.

Myrddin looked directly at Artur.

"Do not leave your visit to Glastonbury too late Artur. We still have much to discuss."

With that, Myrddin turned and departed the presence of the other kings.

Chapter 12

Coventry Castle, Round Court Of Kings

The clearing of Coventry within the Ardu forest had been transformed to a village humming with activity as a great castle was under construction around the site of the Holly Tree.

Midst the din of work and in front of the Holly Tree, was a meeting of the Kings. A perfect circle of stone and around the edge, each king sitting on a stone chair.

"Pray, the workers be given leave for the day," complained Owell Of Glywysing. "I can barely hear myself think."

"Progress waits for no man, my Lord," grinned Gwythyr of Gwent. "Think then this racket is as war Owell of Glywysing and your heart should be soothed."

General laughter.

"Do not tempt me Gwythyr," growled Owell Of Glywysing.

"My Lords," interrupted Artur. "Pray for your forgiveness, but we have much to do and discuss. Here, midst this great circle, we are all equal under the rule of law and safeguarded through sanctuary and honour."

"My Lord Artur," said Atwal of Sealwud, "our people call out asking when shall you bear an heir?"

"The people of Elmet are in union with such sentiment," added Masgwid of Elmet. "When shall you be again wed, my Lord?"

Artur shook his head.

"The matter of matrimony is entirely the provenance of the heart my Lords," smiled Artur embarrassed at the subject.

"Not for a King," said Oswald of Dommoc.

"Certainly not for you King Artur," said Ceowulf of Cent. "All our people pray there be certainty of your legacy."

"Allow me then return the discourse to a different matter my Lords," said Constantine of Alba. "What shall be the law of our union Artur? As an orator, you have the power to unite even the most obstinate of kings. But what of administration of law? For you remain Celt whereas the tribes of Alba and Dumnonia are aligned with the Universal Church, whilst the people of Elmet, Dommoc, Mid Angles and Weald are aligned with the Church of Antioch."

Chapter 12

"We are united by honour," replied Gwynned of Angels. "We are bound by the beliefs of liberty, justice and fraternity, my Lord."

"I do not doubt your character Gwynedd of Angels," said Constantine of Alba, "but these be virtues of heaven, not the laws of men. Without the mortar to bind our kingdoms, I fear our union will not survive a season. What say you Myrddin of Dumnonia?"

Silence as all wait for Myrddin to speak.

"No great union of people has ever been borne without first the unity of common law, of knowledge and culture," said Myrddin. "Yet no civilisation has survived without the honour to virtue and character of men above all things."

"Riddles Myrddin," complained Oswald of Dommoc. "You forever speak in mystery."

"Only for those who are ignorant of the past Oswald of Dommoc," smiled Myrddin.

"Are you calling me ignorant?" growled Oswald of Dommoc.

"I neither cursed nor accused. What you choose to hear or be is your own free will my Lord," replied Myrddin.

"See, this is the problem we have with Catholics," moaned Masgwid of Elmet. "Everything is in riddles."

"I reject that imputation, my Lord," added Constantine of Alba

"They are more like the ancient ways of Celts," said Aelle of Weald. "Never a straight answer."

"My Lords, please," said Artur.

"You set the circle Artur. You said we all have equal right to speak our mind with impunity," said Sigered of Mid Angles. "Do not intrude then to change such promise."

"I challenge any king here, who makes such comparison as the honour of ancients to the mysteries of the Franks," said Owell of Glywysing.

"My Lords, please may we continue?" asked Artur.

The tone rapidly deteriorated as kings were now openly yelling at other kings.

"Do you see the cost of peace Artur?" smiled Myrddin. "Remember, we are but men, not gods."

****

Coventry Castle

A grand spectacle of tents and great bonfires, lit up the walls of a castle still under construction. In front of the unfinished castle, was a great raised platform upon which Artur, Osmond of Wicce, Gwynedd of Angels, Owell of Glywysing and Myrddin of Dumnonia were seated with several others observing and enjoying the festivities.

At the conclusion of a musical piece, Osmond of Wicce stood up and moved toward the front of the stage to the people. Everyone quietened down.

"Tonight we celebrate the most ancient and sacred celebration of Beltaine, watched over by the gods of ancient fertility and prosperity," pronounced Osmond of Wicce. "It be befitting then at this time of rebirth and renewal that our beloved Lord, Artur of Pendraig shall choose a new bride, to bring forth an heir for the people."

Applause from the audience.

"I feel like the prize bull at a Market," whispered Artur to Gwythyr of Gwent.

"That you are my Lord," answered Gwythyr of Gwent.

Artur got up and moved to the front of the stage. He then pointed to Gwynedd to come forward. Gwynedd reluctantly moved to join Artur at the front of the stage.

"While we have lost a great light in Rhodri, we are blessed to have the heart of his son Gwynedd."

Artur then presented a gold shield to Gwynedd.

"Gwynedd of Angels, will you promise to be the Owain and protector of the old ways, the sovereign of our ancient faith in honour, humility and strength?"

Gwynedd looks at first taken aback and then comes and accepts the gold shield.

"With all my heart, my mind and spirit I shall be faithful to the burden you have granted me."

More applause from the crowd as Artur and Gwynedd embrace. As celebrations continued, Artur stood midst the kings and a space made by the crowd in front of him.

Owell of Glywysing now stepped forth into the space.

"My Lord. Let me present my daughter Catrin."

From the back of the crowd, into the space stepped confidently a beautiful young girl. Her head held high.

"An honour to meet you fine maiden."

"You be not as old as I thought you would look my Lord," replied Catrin.

Gasps from some of the audience.

"My apology, my Lord," said Owell of Glywysing. "It is as if the gods played a trick and brought forth the mind of a man in the body of a maiden."

General laughter.

"Never crush such spirit," laughed Artur. "May I ask how such a fine beauty has not yet been betrothed?"

"While I honour my father and house tonight, I be no piece of meat, or prize of property," protested Catrin. "Either I shall find a man as my equal or I shall die alone."

More gasps from the audience as Artur applauds.

"Bravo and spoken like a true Queen, lady Catrin," said Artur.

Catrin blushed as Owell pushed her out of the way, clearly angry at her outbursts. Gwythyr of Gwent now entered the space between the onlookers.

"My Lord, May I present my daughter Gwenhwyfawr."

Suddenly musicians appeared in the space, as a haunting voice came from within the crowd and the onlookers parted to reveal Gwenhwyfawr singing a melodious tune.

All the onlookers as well as Artur are transfixed by both her beauty and her voice. When she finished, she bowed to Artur as rapturous applause reverberated for her song.

"Pray tell me Gwenhwyfawr, how did one come to such beauty of voice and form?" asked Artur.

"My Lord, I know not the mind of the gods, only that we may choose by our own will the destiny set before us," she replied.

"I must confess Gwythyr of Gwent, that I recall seeing from afar such beauty, in less complicated times," said Artur. "But little did I believe that now I would be choosing such potential union under these circumstances."

"My Lord, Gwenhwyfawr is every ounce the strength of a Queen, and personifies the living beauty of our ancestry," smiled Gwythyr proudly.

Artur bowed.

"I thank my fellow kings and their most noble offers of hand in matrimony. Allow me a moment, to reflect whereupon I shall make my announcement."

Later, Myrddin of Dumnonia was speaking with Gwythyr of Gwent as Owell of Glywysing as Catrin approached.

"Lord Myrddin of Dumnonia. An honour," smiled Catrin.

"Please excuse my daughter," said Owell of Glywysing.

Myrddin smiled.

"She is who she is," replied Myrddin. "Come, Catrin. Let us discourse."

Chapter 12

Owell of Glywysing and Gwythyr of Gwent move off warily as Catrin remained with Myrddin of Dumnonia.

"Are you really a magician and great wizard?" she asked him.

Myrddin laughed.

"To some who cannot see what their eyes show them, or hear what their ears tell them. To those who ignore the simple truth that knowledge and ancient wisdom is the greatest of all magic."

"Then show me some magic."

"What do you wish?"

"I have heard you can foretell events in the future, that you are a soothsayer. What then is my future, shall Artur choose me, over that flower?"

"What does your belly tell you?"

"That it is not magic. Anyone who believes in their own intuition can sense these things."

"Yet, how many act on that intuition Catrin?"

Catrin then frowned and looked seriously at Myrddin.

"What then of my future? Will I someday become a great queen?"

The crowd hushed as Artur returned to the stage. Myrddin watched on before turning back to Catrin.

"You will choose to do what your will directs you to do," he smiled to her. "But remember, ultimately in the greatest seasons of good and evil, even evil serves the purposes of the Divine."

Myrddin then left Catrin before moving forward to see the announcement.

Chapter 13

Glastonbury Abbey, Cathedral

The ancient Glastonbury Cathedral was full of people, breathlessly silent. At the altar stood Bishop King Myrddin of Dumnonia in his full vestments. In front of him stood Artur.

Behind him, Artur could hear the murmurs and reactions of the crowd. He turned to watch the bridal procession enter the Cathedral. When the bride arrived, Artur moved over and lifted the veil to reveal the radiant face of Gwenhwyfawr.

****

Pengwern Castle

Outside the castle, celebrations continued, as people cheered and continued to drink and sing.

Within the royal bed chamber, Artur lent his head against the wall near a narrow window to the outside world. He listened to the merriment and music below him. Behind him was Gwenhwyfawr in her night clothes sitting upright in bed.

Gwenhwyfawr got out of bed and came over to Artur.

"My Lord, this be our wedding night, yet you remain elsewhere."

"I am sorry my lady," smiled Artur. "My mind is not my own this night."

Gwenhwyfawr reached over to kiss him, before Artur recoiled to the advance. In shock, she moved away for a moment.

"I accept that I can never live up to the image of your first wife Eadythe taken from you. Yet all I ask my Lord is that you grant me the dignity that this be a consummated matrimony, or else, release me from my vows."

Artur walked over to Gwenhwyfawr, embracing her and stroking her hair.

"My beautiful Gwenhwyfawr. My melancholy chokes your radiance and beauty. Forgive me."

Artur kissed Gwenhwyfawr in a warm embrace as hand in hand they return to the bed.

****

Caerdyf Castle, Glywysing

Chapter 13

The imposing edifice of Caerdyf Castle and the village, the capital of Glywysing.

Within the castle, the body of King Owell of Glywysing lay in state as his children, Gruffydd, Cadwgan and Catrin stand in witness, along with the chief bodyguard of the king (Earin) and the royal guards.

"As King, I shall honour our father with building even a greater city than Caerdyf," proclaimed Gruffydd.

"You oaf! You do not deserve to be king," growled Cadwgan.

"Brothers. Your father is not yet cold but you fight like dogs," moaned Catrin.

"Stand back sister," replied Cadwgan, "lest my blade pierce your heart."

Cadwgan then unsheathed his sword, followed by Gruffydd, and the two brothers began fighting as Catrin and attendants watch, helpless.

"Gruffydd stop this madness!" yelled Catrin, causing Gruffydd to be distracted and look at her. Yet instead of yielding, Gadwgan took the opportunity and drove his sword into the chest of his brother.

Catrin screamed in anger and as Gadwgan was standing half smiling, half in shock, over the body of

Gruffydd, Catrin picked up the sword of Gruffydd and drove it into the chest of Gadwgan.

Gadwgan turned to look at her in shock as Gruffydd closed his eyes and died.

"Damn you Gadwgan," screamed Catrin. "You have killed us all."

Catrin crumpled to the floor sobbing uncontrollably as Earin and the guards move forward to the bodies of dead brothers, lying before their dead father in state. Catrin looked over and ceased sobbing, before composing herself.

"Summons the ministers," said Catrin to Earin. "Call a Council of the chiefs. I am now Queen."

"But you are still a maiden, my lady."

Catrin picked up the sword next to her and moved closer to Earin, revealing to him the bloody tip.

"Do not question me again," she growled menacingly. "I be now Morgan of the Fates, the goddess of the sea and the true queen of this kingdom."

****

Coventry

Chapter 13

The completed Coventry Castle and Coventry village. Within the throne room of the Castle, Artur and Gwenhwyfawr were sitting upon raised thrones as dignitaries and diplomats from various kingdoms and foreign lands make their representations and gifts.

Oddr Sigurdr as head of the royal guard, stood behind and to the side of the throne of Artur.

As each party came forward, the herald (Herald Lochwyn) announced their identity and business. One of those was Catrin.

"My Lord and Lady, Come now Catrin of Glywysing to present herself to you following the death of her father and two brothers in duel," pronounced Herald Lochwyn.

Catrin stepped forward with Earin, her chief of guards.

"I am Catrin Morgan of Morgannag, Queen of my domain," she said resolutely.

"Catrin. I grieved for the loss of your father," said Artur. "He was a dear friend and honourable counsel."

"I did not come for your pity my Lord. You may address me as Lady, or Queen Morgan of Spirits, but not by that name," replied Catrin. "The woman of which you speak is dead."

"No one here judges you harshly in the light of the actions of your brothers," said Artur. "Your assent is lawful and we recognize you as the true heir to the legacy of your father."

"Then I claim the seat of my father at the circle of Kings," continued Catrin.

"A delicate subject my Lady and Queen," said Artur. "The circle, be one of equals."

"Am I not equal by your own words?"

"I vouchsafe for that. But so too be the consent of all other kings."

Catrin laughed.

"From age to age, the fears of men knows no limit," said Catrin. "Woe be the day the prejudice of the sexes be revealed as not Divine, but the weakness of man."

Gwenhwyfawr frowned and leant forward.

"Do you question the integrity of my husband towards the fair sex my lady?" asked Gwenhwyfawr.

"I merely seek guidance my Lady Gwenhwyfawr," smiled Catrin. "Perhaps you can account for a different answer. Why do we not yet have an heir for Mercia? Does the fair queen resist my lord?"

"Now you question my integrity Morgan?" replied Gwenhwyfawr.

Chapter 13

"Your issue is with me Queen Morgan," said Artur. "Not with Gwenhwyfawr."

"Then before all here today, does the great Artur declare his word broken?" smiled Catrin. "If not, the two ladies may discourse as equally as men, without calling upon a master or guardian."

"She is correct Gwenhwyfawr," said Artur. "I withdraw."

"I merely state Gwenhwyfawr that a woman in favour with heaven would have produced for us an heir for all," added Catrin.

"My lord, what do you say to this slur on my character?" demanded Gwenhwyfawr.

Artur shook his head. "She has not lied," he said. "She has spoken the truth as the gods do not yet favour us an heir Gwenhwyfawr."

Gwenhwyfawr got up from her throne and hastily left the room, with Arthur, Catrin and the rest of the dignitaries remaining.

****

Coventry Castle, Royal Chambers

Mercia

Artur entered the royal chambers, where Gwenhwyfawr was being consoled by her ladies in waiting, who cast a disgusted look at the King, before moving away.

"Go away, my Lord. I do not feel kindly to speaking," said Gwenhwyfawr.

"I had to withdraw Gwenhwyfawr," replied Artur. "Else she would have tricked me into breaking my word."

"Then you should not have spoken in haste," sobbed Gwenhwyfawr. "My character before heaven is now in question my Lord. Yet you fancy the musings of Catrin who now calls herself a goddess over my interests."

"You are my Queen."

"Then defend my honour."

"Please Gwenhwyfawr."

****

Coventry Castle

At the gates of Coventry Castle was Gwenhwyfawr, standing barefoot wrapped in a giant shawl. Next to her was a magnificent saddled and robed white horse, held by the Herald Lochwyn. Artur rushed toward them.

"Gwenhwyfawr, what is this madness?" said Artur breathless from running.

"My husband, the king, does not defend me against a curse of heaven. Therefore, I must call upon heaven myself."

"You cannot ride such a horse in this state. I forbid it."

"Then Catrin is right, that you are no different to the tyrant men of ages past, who demand woman serve as lesser mortals, yet do nothing to defend us when called to account."

Gwenhwyfawr took off her shawl to reveal she was completely naked. All the men suddenly turned around as she used steps next to the horse to get on board.

Artur was speechless in shock.

"Do not impede me my king," said Gwenhwyfawr. "If Heaven judges me without blemish, then my honour shall not be taken and no one shall choose to see the Queen in such state. But if the curse of Catrin be true, then I shall be ruined."

Gwenhwyfawr pulled the horse toward the gates as they slowly open.

"Either course, I shall be leaving Coventry to Gwent before the end of the day. Goodbye Artur."

Artur stood stunned at what he was witnessing as the herald escorted the horse out of the gates and toward the main street of Coventry village.

Along the main street of Coventry village were lined guards facing inwards, amidst an assembly of workers, attendants, women and children assembled, waiting to see what event was about to take place.

Slowly, Herald Lochwyn escorted the white horse and Gwenhwyfawr to the top of the street and with the loudest booming voice, cried out:

"Hear Ye, See Ye, Know thee, the lady, is pious before Heaven. And if it be the wish of Heaven to deprive her of the gift of honour, then let the good and virtuous people of Coventry gaze upon her and judge harshly. If not, then turn your back upon those who would blacken her name.

Almost instantly, the people began turning their backs, including the guards as Gwenhwyfawr, naked on the horse, was led by Herald Lochwyn down the street.

As Gwenhwyfawr and the Herald passed building after building the people turned their backs. As they are almost at the end of the road, a young man (Tom) began to turn his head in order to glance. In that instant, he was promptly struck in the face with a broom by a young woman next to him, who had spotted him trying to glance a peek.

"You've blinded me. I cannot see," he yelped.

At the end of the street, the accompanying guards handed Gwenhwyfawr her shawl and a party of her ladies in waiting ride up to console her, before they departed to Gwent.

Mercia

Chapter 14

Coventry Castle

Upon the battlements of Coventry Castle were standing Artur and Gwynedd.

"Gwynedd, I go in the morn to visit Bishop King Myrddin of the Britons at Glastonbury."

"Caution my Lord, replied Gwynedd. "He is known by many as a fearful wizard, who may cast spells even upon the purest heart."

"Superstitions Gwynedd, smiled Artur. "From men who have not seen Glastonbury, nor fully appreciate the Divine nature of this world."

Gwynedd bowed down before Artur.

"What would you have me do my Lord?"

"You are Owain. Guard the covenant, protect the fragile peace and I shall return soon."

****

Glastonbury, Capital of Dumnonia, South West England

Artur arrived with his royal guard to the massive ancient Celtic Glastonbury fortress (Glastonbury Tor) a mile east of Cathedral, dominating the skyline.

There, at the main gate to the fortress, King Myrddin of

Dumnonia was waiting with a cadre of priests to welcome him.

"Welcome to ancient Glastonbury, King Artur," said Myrddin embracing Artur. "I hoped you would come."

"My Lord Myrddin, the knowledge I seek may be even more elusive."

"Have no fear my Lord. You are not the first, nor will you be the last to find yourself in strife with the greater of the sexes."

Myrddin and Artur began walking along a well worn stone path inside the walls of the fortress. Artur looked across at the defence walls and then the main fortress walls. Myrddin smiled.

"A thousand years," said Myrddin. "That is the age of the stones and these walls you now see Artur. One of the seven great fortresses of the ancients. A place sacred for countless generations of Celts and sons and daughters of this great island. Sadly one day nothing will be left after evil will spend two hundred years removing every single stone you see."

Chapter 14

Myrddin pointed to a stone bench in front of them, an ornate gold and wooden box placed in front of the bench.

"Here, I wish to show you something."

They sat down on the stone bench, Artur observing with interest the box in front of them.

"Artur, do you believe in the honour of the ancient ways?" asked Myrddin.

"All my life I have tried to live according to the virtues of our ancestors," replied Artur. "To protect, to provide and to serve."

"This is good," smiled Myrddin.

"Yet I must confess, more recently I have grown sceptical of all religion and their approach to the key answers of life," added Artur.

"Such as the question of why if the Divine is fundamentally good are good people allowed to be taken so terribly?" said Myrddin.

Artur looked shocked and surprised.

"How? how did you know this?"

Myrddin laughed. "Artur, please do not think you are the only man who has ever lost faith upon inadequate answers in the face of tragedy. Nor will you be the last. The sad truth is that all religions fail in many ways to adequately explain the key challenges of life. Instead, they substitute substance too often with ritual or custom. Your beautiful wife and daughter did not die because the Divine Creator specifically willed it. They died because of the consequences of the Divine Gift free will. There is a huge difference."

"I do not fully understand Myrddin."

"Artur, do you still trust the ancient wisdom of your ancestors that showed life and the universe is a dream?"

"Not the same as I used to, but generally yes."

"And can you hold two different thoughts in your mind simultaneously?"

"No, of course not. Once cancels the other."

"And do you believe in the existence of good and evil?"

"Now you are testing my patience."

"Well then, by your own words, you have all the answers to make sense of even the darkest night of the soul. If life and the universe is a dream, then common sense demands that the Divine Creator can never directly intervene in the affairs of humanity, as some would claim. Such an act would destroy the dream and existence. So, instead form within the dream is granted certain autonomy and life is granted free will - the consequence being the presence of good and evil. Do you now see?"

Artur smiled. "Yes, I see what you mean. Thank you. Thank you for giving me an understanding."

"You are welcome," smiled Myrddin. "So tell me Artur, what do you know of the origins of our ancient law and indeed Tara?"

"My father and my tutors taught me that this was the home of the gods and their laws, but that in war it was destroyed."

"Artur, Tara was a real place and fortress in Ireland, eighteen miles north west of Dublin, in the shape of a great shield nearly two miles across from side to side formed more than forty two generations ago by a great prophet called Jeremiah."

"Yes, I have heard of him," said Artur.

"Jeremiah was from a famous line of Holly priests that returned to Egypt and the Island of the Elephant and became great soothsayers and teachers. They were the teachers of Pharoahs and princes of Egypt.

"Yes, I have heard of Egypt and Pharaohs.

"Long ago, the Egyptians held that heaven and earth was bound by a sacred connection, the tree of life, the Kabala. But this bond was broken because of the reign of false kings. So in Ireland, Jeremiah recreated the Tree of Life from Dublin north-east one hundred and twenty three miles to Inishmurray Island. Tara was a key centre of this new connection between Heaven and Earth, as was the monasteries of Clones, Armagh, Kells, Legan, Ballinamore and Conmacnoise."

"Why did Jeremiah come to Ireland?" asked Artur.

"Because he fled from Palestine to Ireland after the Babylonian king Nebuchadnezzar destroyed Jerusalem and killed the last messiah king of the Yahudi. So to Ireland he brought the last living bloodline through Princess Tamar Tephi as well as many sacred objects."

"I heard these myths in my childhood," said Artur.

"They are not myths Artur."

"Let me show you."

Myrddin got up and moved over to the locked ornate gold box. He opened it to reveal a magnificent sword.

"It is extraordinary," said Artur. "Beautiful."

"Pick it up,"smiled Myrddin.

Artur picked up the sword out of the box and was stunned when the sword seemed to have a vibratory force.

"You can feel that force can't you?" asked Myrddin.

"I feel it in my hand and my arm, like a great strength," said Artur. "What magic this be Myrddin?"

Chapter 14

"No Persian magic trick Artur. A divine gift. Ex Caeli Bur, The Sword from Heaven. Harpe Da Vide, The Sword of Destiny and Foresight. The Sword of Kings. Forged by the greatest Holly smiths of Ireland and given as the symbol of rule of Pharaoh of Egypt many generations before even the messiah kings of the Yahudi. The Romans sacrificed many dozens of legions in search of what you hold in your hand."

"You say this to be Ex Caeli Bur, The Sword from Heaven?"

"You tell me Artur," said Myrddin. "Your eyes tell you what they see is perfect steel, without a single blemish, even after a thousand battles. You feel it in your body, your belly and your heart, yet your mind doubts."

"Why then be this in your possession?"

"What do you know of Glastonbury, Artur?"

"A place of great sacredness, even if it now be Christian."

"Artur, kingdoms and civilizations are like forests. They grow, they live and die till men no longer remember. This be not the first time. But no people were saved just by looking backwards. Jeremiah knew this and the thirty second holly priest known as Yahusiah knew this."

"Whom?"

"The son of Mariah, the only woman to be a true prophetess of Yaihu and the Crown Prince of the Holly, Joseph A Rama Theo, His Divine Highness. You know him as the saviour Jesus Christ."

"I came with respect to this place and your name my Lord. Not to be converted," frowned Artur, as Myrddin laughed.

"Would you like to see where the young Yahusiah, also known as Jesus, spent his years from the age of three until ten, before returning with his father Holly King Joseph A Rama Theo to the great city King Joseph built in Palestine called Sepphoris?"

"Here?"

Myrddin got up and walked with Artur to the entrance of the main fortress. They walked up a stone staircase into a great room, full of tens of thousands of books and manuscripts.

"Here be the true records of our species and all ancient civilisations. The soul of wisdom of the Cuilliaéan. The very thing you say you honour, yet do not through your ignorance. Here, many a great man learnt the mind of the Divine, including the one whom they now call Jesus Christ."

Artur shook his head as he continued to hold Ex Caeli Bur.

"I do not know what to say. I have no words to describe such a place that you now show me," he said. "Everything that I was told was untrue."

Myrddin smiled.

"Do not be troubled Artur. Reality be thought, dream and vision. The illusion is thinking that stones and these books can have some permanence. You have a good heart Artur, yet know nothing of its cause, nor yet of your destiny."

Mercia

Chapter 15

Coventry Castle, Round Court Of Kings

The circle of Kings sat in the completed courtyard surrounding the Holly Tree within the Coventry Castle. Catrin of Morgannag now sat in the place of her father.

"My fellow Kings and Queen. Forgive me," said Artur. "For you have shown me my error."

General mumbling until Artur raised his hand.

"No it is true," he continued. "I am neither the scholar nor father that our fragile peace demands. Yet as a warrior, I now see the enemy more clearly. Not in flesh and bone and iron, but in what becomes the ideas and symbols of our destiny."

"Now you truly do speak in the riddles of Myrddin my Lord," said Oswald of Dommoc.

"Oswald of Dommoc, I pray you and all here present allow me to finish," replied Artur. "For it is your right to affirm or deny what I am about to speak. A people without trust or virtue are abandoned to the storm of chaos and cannot survive. Yet a people cannot hold by honour and trust alone. We must have one common form of law. More, we must have one common name for our united kingdoms. More, we must have symbols for such union that will outlast one king, one queen, one house."

"What then do you propose Artur?" asked Constantine of Alba.

"Whether Celt, Christian or Universal Church, all are bound by the golden rule that none are above the law, that justice be fair, without fear or favour," said Artur. "Let then the scholars decide therefrom."

"And of name, what do you propose?" asked Aelle of Weald.

"Do we all not agree this island be named by the Romans as Britannia?" continued Artur. "From which we did see briefly the unity of the Britons. Therefore, let our united kingdoms be known as Great Britain."

"We be Christian first and foremost Artur," added Masgwid of Elmet. "Our people respect and welcome one common law, but cannot abide by serving a pagan united kingdom against our faith."

"Nor Masgwid of Elmet would the people of Morgannag serve by the edicts of Antioch," growled Catrin of Morgannag.

"My lady you may occupy such seat," replied Masgwid of Elmet coldly, "but that grants you no right to speak so."

Catrin stood up, followed by Masgwid and Aelle of Weald and several others. Artur waved his hands that they sit back down.

"My Lords. My Lords and lady," said Artur. "Do not let this moment be lost. Stay firm to the cause and history."

"A miracle Lord Artur," added Ceowulf of Cent. "Else the circle cannot hold."

"A symbol perhaps?" asked Myrddin.

"What symbol?" replied Bleddri of Dyfed.

Artur reached back to his attendant and unsheathed Ex Caeli Bur before all the kings. A collective gasp.

"Is that what I think it be?" stuttered Bleddri of Dyfed.

"It is Ex Caeli Bur, the Sword of Heaven," said Artur. "It is Harpe Da Vide, The Sword of Destiny and Foresight. The Sword of Kings. Forged by the greatest Holly smiths of Ireland and given as the symbol of rule of law."

Artur thrust the sword high into a beam of light so that the blade caught it, causing the light to be split into a thousand beams around the room. At that moment the kings, including Catrin of Morgannag and even Myrddin got off from their stone thrones and knelt before Artur now at the centre of the circle.

"Upon the grace of heaven, the gift of Ex Caeli Bur and my honour, I promise to all present that I shall never permit arms to be raised against any king to king," said Artur. "And by the blessing of Heaven we shall form the united kingdom of Great Britain, not under the dragon, but the symbol of the lion and the sword of justice. I shall yield to the authority of the Universal Church by investiture and coronation and come what may, though the heavens fall, let justice for all our people be done!"

****

Coventry Castle, Battlements

Upon the battlements of Coventry Castle stood Artur, looking out at the setting sun over the tops of the forest. Catrin of Morgannag approached him and placed her hand on his shoulder before Artur turned around, surprised it was her.

"Queen Morgannag."

Catrin bowed.

Chapter 15

"I would not have believed today if not for my own eyes my Lord."

"What will be, will be my lady."

"Forgive me my Lord for my quick temper and artful tongue. I did not mean to cause you such distress."

"You were right to chastise me," he smiled. "Heaven and the law demands we be equal. Yet you demonstrated by your courage this be not the practice by what did you say? Fearful men?"

"Weak men. Something, you my Lord are not."

Catrin moved closer to Artur and gently touched his arm and chest.

"It is not right that you be alone my Lord. Nor you be without heir."

"All I have is my word and character. Nothing more."

"If heaven did not want it so, then it would not be, my Lord."

Catrin moved to kiss Artur just as Gwynned of Angels appeared on the battlements. Catrin is the first to sense his presence and instinctively stepped back to a safe distance.

"Gwynned," she smiled.

Gwynned bowed.

"My lord, my lady," he said.

"Excuse me my Lords, interrupted Catrin. "I must return to Caerdyf."

Both Artur and Gwynedd bow to Catrin as she departed from the battlements.

"My Lord you called for me? asked Gwynedd.

"Gwynedd, there be a great battle within the heavens and upon the earth, for which the prize is nothing less than the soul of mankind. And we are not without cause to its outcome."

"What would you have me do my Lord?" asked Gwynedd.

"Gwynedd, you are Owain. You are a great king. I have a further burden to give to you."

Artur revealed from his scabbard Ex Caeli Bur, the Sword of Heaven. At one look, Gwynedd dropped to his knees.

"No Gwynedd. Please arise."

Artur handed Ex Caeli Bur to Gwynedd.

"Only a man of pure heart or Cuilliaéan may hold the sword of destiny," smiled Artur. "You be both."

"My Lord. It is you who truly are the King of Kings and our saviour."

"But it is you Gwynedd who shall be known as the purified holder of the Sword and the Lancea Lot, not

I," replied Artur. "You are borne of the Holly priest lines and it is you who is destined to save the world from darkness."

"My Lord, how can I accept such burden as the Lancea Lot? How shall such things come to pass?"

"Myrddin showed to me the grave danger of the Holy Grail, the Holly Blood, the Sangreal of Europa in Emperor Charles of the Franks. His is the last Holly blood of Europa. If he be snuffed out, then a great period of evil shall descend upon the lands of Europa for a great many years. Men will rise even worse than the Persian and Amorican merchants."

"As you command," said Gwynedd, "so shall I obey."

"Then you shall go upon this sacred quest Gwynedd Lancelot. Go with our Army to the land of the Franks and make it known to all the enemies of light, that they shall not succeed.

****

Coventry Castle, Kings Quarters

Inside his bedroom, Artur slowly finished removing the last of his garments. As he turned, he stopped for a moment in front of a full length mirror and glanced at himself and the scars upon his arms and torso. There was a knock on the door, before it opened. "Thank you but I am fine," he said without turning around.

As he heard the door close, Artur stared for a few more moments into the mirror. A face almost as if a stranger. A face that could not hide the sadness and loneliness of loss and regrets.

Yet when Artur turned to go to bed, there in front of him was Catrin of Morgannag standing only in a night gown.

"I can leave if you wish, my Lord," she said softly. "But I cannot hide any more my pain or my feelings."

Artur moved over to her.

"No, we have both suffered greatly Catrin. But, even so I -"

Catrin put her finger to his lips to stop him speaking and then kissed him passionately, and they embraced. Whilst still in passionate embrace, Artur and Catrin fell onto the bed.

Chapter 16

Glastonbury Abbey, Cathedral, Christmas Day 888 CE

At the central altar of Glastonbury Cathedral stood Bishop King Myrddin, wearing ornate vestments and mitre hat. Throughout the cathedral stood a congregation of kings and leaders from the known world, while Gwynedd stood to the side of the altar with Ex Caeli Bur sheathed.

At the entrance to the Cathedral, stood Artur barefoot in a simple white garment. Slowly and methodically, Artur walked along the aisle toward the altar and Myrddin. Before the altar he stopped bowing his head.

"Halt. Who enters the most sacred sanctuary of Divine presence?" proclaimed Myrddin.

"It is I, the man and transgressor Artur of Pendraig as a true penitent who comes before these witnesses to most humbly petition Heaven and the Divine Creator for forgiveness and mercy."

"Then kneel Artur of Pendraig, that we may first examine your conscience and character."

Artur stepped forward and knelt on a hard stone before Myrddin.

"Before the almighty Creator of the Universe, all the angels and saints of Heaven and all here present, do you Artur of Pendraig promise to speak only the truth and honour the binding of your word?"

"I promise."

"And do you promise to be faithful, loyal trustworthy and dependable to the one true and holy universal church?"

"I promise."

"And do you promise to be courageous and strong in defending all of the people of your domain?"

"I promise."

"And do you promise to respect and protect the rule of law, fairness and equality of all?"

"I promise."

"And do you promise to self restraint, frugality and humility?"

"I promise."

"And do you promise to the gift of charity and alms to those in need?"

"I promise."

"And do you promise to the acts of mercy, compassion and forgiveness of others, as you yourself are forgiven?"

"I promise."

"Then Artur of Pendraig upon your solemn oaths to the true sacraments of the Universal Church, seven times seven, your transgressions be forgiven."

Myrddin made the sign of the cross above the head of Artur, before continuing.

"Verily, I bring unto you a heavy burden in the form of a Divine Commission from Heaven that no man, lest he be a true penitent of good character, may receive."

An attendant stepped forward with a small jar. Myrddin tipped the jar so that some oil came onto his right hand. He then placed the oil in the sign of a cross upon the forehead of Artur.

"By the most sacred oil of the Holly Christ, your body is consecrated and by this seal your spirit is anointed that no man, or woman or spirit may defy Heaven as to the granting of your divine gift as a saviour to the people and their true Sovereign."

Myrddin stepped back as attendants moved closer.

"Arise Artur of Pendraig."

Mercia

Artur stood up as attendants step over and placed red slippers on his feet and then cover him in beautiful gold and red and blue coloured vestments, including gold cord tied around his waste. Myrddin then placed a crown upon the head of Artur.

"This crown be a constant symbol of your Divine and Apostolic commission and for all your rightful heirs and successors."

Myrddin then handed Artur a gold orb with a cross upon it. Artur accepted it and placed it in his left hand.

"This sacred globe be a symbol of your lawful custody and possession as wise steward of all land and all the fruits of the land of the Island of Britain from the furthest shores to the north, to the south, to the west and to the east of the domain known as the Kingdom of Great Britain."

Myrddin then nodded to Gwynedd who came forward and unsheathed Ex Caeli Bur as there was a collective gasp from those in attendance. Gwynedd handed it to Myrddin who then handed Artur the sword which he grasped in his right hand.

"This be the sacred sword of destiny, the true sword of King David of the Yahudah, the sword that has never been removed from the foundation of the Holly until now. You must choose King Artur, whether you shall rule by the sword, or by the rule of law?"

"I choose to rule by law not by force or fear," said Artur.

"Then Heaven ordains you shall be a just king," replied Myrddin.

Myrddin removed the Ex Caeli Bur from Artur and handed it back to Gwynedd as an attendant handed Myrddin a gold Sceptre which Myrddin then gave to Artur.

"By this rod of law, you Artur of Pendraig shall become the living law. That what you speak is law."

Myrddin then turned to the audience.

"Heaven and the Divine Creator has ordained this man be worthy as the first and true king of the realm of Great Britain. Yet no king may rule without also the consent of the people. What say you? Shall you elect Artur to be your king?"

"Long live King Artur! Long live King Artur! Long live King Artur! Long live King Artur!"

****

Glastonbury Abbey

Artur stood outside of the Abbey, next to Myrddin and Gwynedd, surrounded by continued rapturous applause when Queen Catrin of Morgannag came up to him and bowed.

"Your majesty," she smiled. "On such an illustrious day, where be your Queen?"

"Queen Morgan, this be not the time or the place," replied Artur, as Myrddin looked at her strangely.

"When shall that be your majesty? We were sorely interrupted. For my people pledge their undying loyalty to Great Britain, yet we cry out for a rightful heir."

"A subject where I see that you have more than a personal interest," smiled Myrddin to Catrin, causing both Artur and Catrin of Morgannag to look at him strangely.

"More riddles Myrddin," snapped Catrin of Morgannag.

Myrddin shrugged his shoulders.

"I may of course be mistaken my lady, but it seems you have a deep and abiding fulsome glow about you, yet as much as you hide your beautiful frame by your garments."

Artur turned bright red, as Queen Catrin of Morgannag and everyone waited upon his reply.

Chapter 16

"Fate then shall decide the answer my lady," said Artur. "For I will die wedded to Gwenhwyfawr, even if I die alone."

The face of Catrin changed to cold rage as she bowed her head.

"Then fate shall indeed decide your majesty."

Mercia

Chapter 17

Veneti Fortress, Brittany, Capital of Exiled Amoricans

A small fishing port and a rudimentary fortress on the Brittany coastline. Inside a room of the fortress was a great library, filled with manuscripts. Within the room, Ælfred was dressed in much simpler and austere clothing, listening to a scholar (Asser) as he spoke while another learned looking man (Nennius) looked on. In the background were several desks of scribes writing and copying texts.

"And then Lord Artur took his son Amur to a stone altar in the field and then slaughtered his son as but a sacrifice of a mere creature to his Christian god," recited Asser.

"Fantastic Asser," beamed Ælfred. "See Nennius, we need more excitement in your work. It is too boring."

"Even I would struggle with such claims, my Lord," said Nennius. "Alas, no one will believe them."

At that moment, Ætheling appeared into the room and bowed.

"What news of Gwynedd the Lancelot and the Army of Great Britain?" asked Ælfred.

"My lord ten thousand have arrived and been six days now in Paris," replied Ætheling. "So many ships, you could walk from Paris to the coast. The largest standing army in all of Europe. Emperor Charles of the Franks has embraced the show of strength and Rudolph the Welf of Burgundy has withdrawn his troops."

"I would still back my new army of scholars and money lenders any day Ætheling," grinned Ælfred. "People are more inclined to believe an outrageous lie than a boring truth. So what then of Artur?"

"My lord, Queen Gwenhwyfawr remains at Casenwydd in Gwent with her young son and Artur at Coventry," replied Ætheling.

"My lord, Queen Gwenhwyfawr remains at Casenwydd in Gwent with her young son and Artur at Coventry," replied Ætheling.

Ælfred rubbed his chin as Ætheling continued.

"And I have on sound authority that Queen Morgan of Morgannag is withdrawing her troops from the Great Army on account of a feud with Artur."

Ælfred laughed as he got up from his chair and started to pace the room.

Chapter 17

"Finally Ætheling, it is our time to return and visit the fair Queen of Morgannag," he said. "Prepare the ships."

Ætheling nodded and departs the room. Ælfred turned to Asser and Nennius

"Dear Asser and Nennius," smiled Ælfred, "you have taught me well these years of exile. I care not now who claims to be king, only that we control the coin and the records of history."

****

Caerdyf Castle, Morgannag

Caerdyf fishing village, and hanging like a spectre over it, stood Caerdyf Castle. Inside the castle, Queen Catrin of Morgannag was sitting on the throne, suckling a young blonde haired boy, with her ladies in waiting dressed as fairies at her feet.

Around the throne room, her guards wore ornamental helmets of rams heads, giving the impression of demonic attendants as Ælfred, Æthelbal and Ætheling entered. Upon observing the guards the Amoricans initially look apprehensive.

Mercia

"The Great Ælfred has returned from hiding!" yelled Catrin, stopping her son from suckling and removing him from her lap. One of her ladies in waiting, dressed as a fairy, gently took his arm and helped him walk down and sit to the side of his mother.

Ælfred smiled and bowed.

"Impressive your majesty. We come in peace and to honour your heir with gifts," said Ælfred, snapping his fingers and causing two attendants to come forward with a small suit of gold armour and a small chest of glass bottles. "I pray you tell us the name of your fine son?"

"Mordred. The one who shall bring death and destruction to all that defy our will."

"Ah, excellent," replied Ælfred. "Then please accept these humble tokens. A suit of armour made by the finest craftsmen and potions from the most ancient of sorcerers and doctors of North Africa."

Catrin signalled her attendants to bring the gifts closer so she could admire them, as her son Mordred got to his feet and ran over to look.

"He is a handsome boy, your Majesty, of four years?"

"Three," said Catrin.

"His father must be proud," smiled Ælfred.

"Careful Amorican," growled Catrin. "I be less slow and forgiving than the Normans."

"Your majesty, I have not come to fight or to insult but to inquire as to your proposed action to punish King Artur for his transgressions against you?"

"What business is it of yours merchant? To profit on the misery and division of others? I bear no grudge against Artur."

"My great apology then my Queen. It be Gwenhwyfawr who is in error."

"Indeed the miscreant is at fault. Yet you shall not succeed in cleaving my loyalty."

"What then your legacy my Queen? asked Ælfred smiling at Mordred. "For when Artur falls because of the slight by Gwenhwyfawr to deprive him an heir, so too does Great Britain and any legitimate claim. Am I wrong in assuming by your own law, bastards do not count?"

"You enrage me Amorican. I warn you most gravely."

"How then may I help resolve such rage my Queen, towards those who are responsible for such doom? "

"And in return?" said Catrin.

Mercia

"Forgive me if I have offended you in any way oh great Queen. We be but humble merchants, nothing more. All we seek is free trade and to help others."

Catrin laughed. "It is true that I am bound in passion to the darkest knowledge of magic and taboo. But you - your cold heart makes me look as if I be unblemished. Truly, there be no greater wickedness or evil than your business of money lending, slavery, arms and addictions."

Ælfred smiled. "I take no offence my Queen. It is refreshing to find such intellect. Now that there is no misunderstanding, I take it we can be of some service."

Chapter 18

Casnewydd, Capital of Gwent, Southern Wales

Casnewydd, the capital of Gwent as a force of several hundred soldiers of Morgannag move forward towards the largely undefended castle. Inside the castle, Gwythyr of Gwent and several guards stood defiantly as Queen Catrin Morgannag accompanied by the head of her guard (Earin) and her ram helmeted guards storm the main hall and seize Gwythyr, immediately killing his guards.

"This is an outrage Morgan. You have no right."

Queen Catrin Morgannag moved forward and thrust her sword into Gwythyr of Gwent, who fell to the ground.

"Spare me the speech Gwythyr, I am in haste."

Catrin Morgannag moved to the end of the hall and the doorway to the passages.

"Have the men find her," she commanded to Earin. "Before she escapes. But no one is to harm her."

Earin and the men fan out throughout the castle.

****

Mercia

Casnewydd Castle, Throne Room

Queen Catrin Morgannag sat on the Gwent throne as her guards brought out Gwenhwyfawr.

"Queen Gwenhwyfawr, my absent Queen."

"Soon, you shall be punished for what you have done."

"So shall you my Queen. So shall you."

"In the meantime as my guest at Caerdyf, we can discourse of what might have been. "

Catrin signalled to the guards and they take Gwenhwyfawr away, leaving Queen Catrin Morgannag with Earin.

Slowly she lifted herself off the throne and took one last look.

"Burn it. Burn it all."

****

Coventry Castle

Coventry Castle, lit by the watch fires of night. Inside, Artur was sitting in the throne room as papers and documents were presented to him, when Herald Lochwyn rushed in.

"Your majesty. Catrin of Morgannag has slain Gwythyr of Gwent and taken Queen Gwenhwyfawr as hostage."

Artur got up from the throne and started pacing.

"Shall we now summons the Lancelot and the army to return from Europa, my Lord?"

Artur shook his head.

"That is exactly what Queen Morgan wants us to do. Return the army and it will quickly dissolve back into the militia of kings and warlords. Besides, I made a solemn vow to Myrddin to protect the last Holly Sangreal (Holy Grail) of the Franks."

"But my Lord, the Emperor Charles is dead. And his son Bernard is too weak to lead, whereas Gwenhwyfawr is your Queen."

"Held by a member of the circle of Kings and Queens of Great Britain. If I move against Queen Morgan myself, not only do I dissolve the kingdom, I destroy myself."

"What then shall be done?" asked Herald Lochwyn.

"Pray and wait. "

Mercia

Chapter 19

Caerdyf Castle, Morgannag

Within Caerdyf Castle, the Royal Chambers were decorated like some other worldly tale, with the attendant guards like goblins in their rams head helmets and the ladies in waiting like fairies.

Queen Catrin of Morgannag was sitting now in a soft flowing dress as the ladies brush the blonde hair of her son Mordred, while Gwenhwyfawr was also in a soft flowing dress, looking desperately uncomfortable as her hair was also being brushed by the ladies.

"Why do men make us hate so?" asked Catrin

Catrin did not respond, but smiled awkwardly.

"We are the most beautiful of all women through the great island, yet here we are, preparing to die," continued Catrin.

Mordred looked at her strangely. "Am I going to die mummy?" he asked.

Catrin laughed. "No, not you my beautiful son, she said. "No you will live and reign for a hundred years!"

"It does not have to be so," said Gwenhwyfawr.

"No Gwenhwyfawr, the gods ordained this terrible curse the moment Artur had to choose," said Catrin. "I confess, my rage and hatred blinded me against you. I had thought a thousand times, how I might inflict terrible pain and agony upon you. But I forgive you, as now, I see we are victims to a fate caused by the fear of men as little boys."

"Then why not release me," said Gwenhwyfawr. "You have caused me enough pain."

"Even if I were to release you Gwenhwyfawr, all you would do is continue to try and run away from that inevitable hand which touches all mortal form."

"No, Let us then at least enjoy our beauty together, for the briefest of moments," smiled Catrin. "Until the pipes cry and drums call our day of destiny."

****

Paris

Gwynedd was standing with his younger brother Anarawd overlooking Paris as a messenger hands him a note.

Gwynedd opened it and briefly read the letter, before he threw it on letter on the ground.

Anarawd picked it up and started reading.

Chapter 19

"He still won't recall us. His Queen is hostage and still he will not move."

"He has his reasons," said Anarawd.

"And I have mine my brother that I honour my pledge to him. But when will heaven break this impasse? Something must come to end this purgatory!"

****

London

Upon the Thames were the ships of the Amoricans flying their flags. Inside the main hall of Londonium Castle, Ælfred Æthelbal and Ætheling celebrate their return.

"It is good to be home," proclaimed Ælfred.

"For how long?" asked Ætheling.

"Spare me such gloom," frowned Ælfred. "Artur is a broken man. He cannot move against Queen Morgan and her fairies. He knows that when the army returns, the kingdom is finished and the Celts will return to killing one another, or Normans and we are back in business."

"Yet what if Gwynedd the Lancelot can hold the army together?" asked Ætheling. "What if the Celts and Normans hold for one last moment against Londonium?"

"Then pray the history and brilliant fiction of Nennius and Assur correct a wasted life," replied Ælfred.

****

Coventry Castle

Coventry Castle, with less life, less movement, less joy. At the Round Court of Kings, sitting alone in the stone circle of kings was the solitary figure of Artur looking much older and thinner.

Artur looked up as Myrddin approached.

"Myrddin, what do I do? All I am as king is my word. If this be lost, then I am nothing."

"Such is the burden of a true sovereign, your majesty."

Myrddin sat down on a stone throne opposite Artur.

"Each of us carry our own cross and suffering. Mine is both the gift and curse of foresight and free will. I can foresee the possibilities of the future that character so often prove true. Yet I cannot force any man or woman to change their will."

"I, for example have foreseen my own demise, by the misfortune of drowning."

As Myrddin continues to speak, scenarios are revealed of how Myrddin may drown, the first being slipping upon a washing pool.

"A far less heroic and noble death I admit than others. Yet just as final. Shall it be by slipping upon a pool for washing?"

The second scenario of Myrddin drowning by falling into the sea.

"Shall it be by misfortune of misstep upon the shoreline?"

The third scenario of Myrddin slipping on icy stones and hitting his head upon the edge of a shallow pond then drowning.

"Or something purely mundane in its happenstance?"

Myrddin got up from the stone throne and walked directly over to Artur.

"What I do know Artur is that your story will outlast the kings and queens yet to come. Your heroics in life and death will be the fuel of legend. That not even the most dedicated efforts by men of ill intent to hide the light and truth of your honour will prevail."

Myrddin placed his hands on the shoulders of Artur.

"But as the Universe always demands. By your free will, you must choose to do something."

Chapter 20

London Castle, Throne Room

Ælfred is deeply engaged with his main scribes Nennius and Asser as Ætheling entered the room.

"My Lord, you were mistaken," he moaned. "The Lancelot returns with full force to Londonium this day."

Ælfred looked surprisingly calm.

"So be it. I shall not run. My fate be sealed," said Ælfred.

Ælfred got up and embraced Nennius

"Go now, and may your works be preserved for all the ages beyond these times."

Ælfred then embraced Asser

"Thank you my friend."

"My Lord I promise you," said Asser, "it is you who shall be remembered as the first great king."

Ælfred smiled before looking at Ætheling.

"Take the best men and see our scribes and moneylenders secure their escape," he said. "I shall presently go to greet our coming guests."

Mercia

Ætheling bows and departs with Nennius, Asser and the rest of the scribes and money lenders in the room, leaving Ælfred momentarily alone.

****

London, Docks

Ælfred stood on the banks of the Thames, as the sight of a flood of ships, bearing the symbol of the rampant lion of Great Britain came into vision.

At the Docks, in front of a failed escape vessel, Ælfred stood encircled by armed Norman and Celt warriors. A huge crowd of Londoners looked on. A path between the crowd and the guards separated and Gwynedd the Lancelot appeared in the circle.

"It ends here," said Gwynedd.

"You are mistaken Lancelot. This is where is begins."

"Why did you not try to run away?"

"Why did you break your word to Artur to return to kill me and try to save Gwenhwyfawr? We are who we are."

"We are nothing alike," growled Gwynedd. "You are a man who believes in nothing. A shape shifter, a hollow soul."

"History will judge differently. It will be you, who will be the lesser, whereas I will be glorified as the first true king of all Britain."

"Truth outlasts," said Gwynedd.

"Not if in the future, everyone is a slave of my descendents."

"You have no progeny."

"No?" smiled Ælfred . "Yet you cleaved them in Paris, just as you cleaved them in the streets of London. Yet there are more than you can count. You see poor Lancelot, every merchant that enslaves, that cheats, that robs your precious people is a beloved of mine. And there is nothing you can do to stop it."

"That is where you are wrong," smiled Gwynedd. "Every lie, by its very nature is forced to be the harbinger of truth. A guest that threatens to burn down such a flimsy house when exposed to sufficient light."

"Very well, we shall see if such a bringer of light foretold ever comes," grinned Ælfred. "Meantime, such be my fate, then what honour to be killed by the swift strike of Ex Caeli Bur, the sword of heaven."

Lancelot looked around him and signalled for two of the guard to step away, revealing an opening to the crowd of Londoners behind.

"No blood so corrupted and tainted as yours shall touch the Ex Caeli Bur. Your fate rests in the hands of a jury of your peers. They shall therefore decide your fate," said Gwynedd. "Let twelve of the people come forth."

From the opening of the crowd came twelve souls, from old to young, from male to female into the circle.

"Here are your judges from heaven Ælfred. If you are to be forgiven, then they shall release you. If they deem your crimes most grave, then they shall judge so justly."

Gwynedd then turned and exited from the gap in the circle as the jury of twelve souls encircled Ælfred.

"No! Please I beg you," screamed Ælfred.

Gwynedd continued moving his way through the crowd, as in the background the screams and cries of Ælfred fell silent.

Chapter 21

Caerdyf Castle, Royal Chambers

Queen Catrin of Morgannag in soft feminine dress was knitting with the attendants as Gwenhwyfawr was also knitting opposite her. Earin, her head of guards entered in his full battle armour and bowed to Catrin.

"My Queen, The Lancelot is here, with the army," he said.

Queen Catrin sighed and looked over at Gwenhwyfawr, before putting down the knitting.

"Sister, that day we feared the most has finally come," smiled Catrin. "Let us pray those we love will not abandon us by their absence."

****

Caerdyf, Morgannag

Gwynedd the Lancelot and the mass of the army of Great Britain approached Caerdyf Castle.

Queen Morgan now in her battle armour, stepped out onto the battlements, accompanied by her son Mordred, dressed in his armour of gold.

She surveyed the massive army approaching her castle, as a lone figure of Gwynedd the Lancelot pierced the ranks and approached on horse to within the base of the battlements.

"Release Queen Gwenhwyfawr and on my word, you shall live," he yelled.

"Pray, my Lord the Lancelot, why I would wish to live in the Catholic world of Great Britain, when my heart is with Mercia?"

"You cannot succeed," yelled Gwynedd. "For the second time, release the Queen and you shall not be harmed."

"I do not need to live to succeed," shouted Catrin. "In any event, save your breadth for your king has finally come."

Gwynedd turned to see the spectacle of Artur in his armour, surrounded by flag bearing horsemen riding through the ranks of the army. Cheers spontaneously erupted, including the pipers into a thundering crescendo as Gwynedd withdrew to meet Artur.

****

Gwenhwyfawr, now dressed beautifully like a Queen was escorted out by guards onto the battlements next to Queen Morgan and Mordred in their armour. Catrin extended her hand to her.

"See my Queen. Our savior has finally come."

Gwenhwyfawr approached the stonework and looked out at the figure of Artur riding through the ranks of the army, the sound of the shouts and cries of joy, mixed with the pipers and drums. She lets out a shout of joy herself, before composing herself quickly.

****

As Artur approached, Gwynedd dismounted and knelt, head bowed. Artur dismounted and stepped over to him, looking tired and old.

"My lord, forgive me," said Gwynedd.

"You my friend are the heart of the people," smiled Artur. "You are their conscience. It is I who must apologize to you for forcing you to choose between your heart and soul."

"I have failed to persuade her," said Gwynedd.

"It is not you she calls. Arise Gwynedd."

Gwynedd got up and Artur put his hand on his shoulder.

"You are my true heir. Protect and Defend the People. Protect and Defend the Law. Serve the People."

"My lord. You are the king."

"Who must do his duty," smiled Artur. "For which I call on you indulgence."

Gwynedd handed over Ex Caeli Bur to Artur who smiled once more, before returning to his horse and then turning towards the battlements of the castle.

****

The solitary figure of King Artur approached the base of the battlements of Caerdyf Castle.

As Artur moved close enough that he could see their faces clearly, he nodded from his horse to Gwenhwyfawr and then to Queen Morgan.

"I am here now Queen Morgan. You have my attention."

"So much for your word to the kings," shouted Catrin.

"I did not call upon the army. It is you who broke the peace and summonsed the judgment of Gwynedd the Lancelot."

"I am Morgan, Queen and Goddess of the Sea," screamed Catrin.

"Catrin, your quarrel is with me, not with Gwenhwyfawr. Release her, she has done no harm."

"On the contrary my Lord. I have forgiven Gwenhwyfawr. But it is you who refuses to release her."

Catrin pushed Mordred to the edge of the battlements, so Artur could see him. "Behold my Lord, Mordred, your beautiful son and heir," she said.

Mordred pointed at Artur down below. "Is that my father?"

Catrin nodded her head. "Yes, it is."

Artur bowed his head and began weeping. "Forgive me my Queens, for failing you both."

"Damn you!" screamed Catrin. "For dooming our kingdoms to faded memories. For forcing me to this place."

Artur looked up, his face lined with tears. "What then be your demands Queen Morgan, so that Gwenhwyfawr be free?"

"There is no other way, replied Catrin. "Meet me upon the field and if I am victorious, then your son be consummated by blood as rightful heir. If not, then I am dead and Gwenhwyfawr shall be set free from her bonds."

"My lady, I cannot fight you."

"I am more than your match my old king."

Artur dropped his head.

"I know your mind is made. So it is said. So let it be!"

Catrin watched as Artur turned around and rode away. She then lent down to her son and kissed his forehead, before hugging him.

"Goodbye my son. Be brave. The fiercest gods and demons shall protect you, because I will never leave you."

Chapter 22

Caerdyf Castle

As the afternoon sun filtered through the flags, masses of soldiers watched in front of the castle and upon the battlements, Artur and Catrin squared off with each other, swords drawn.

"Let us dance my lord," smiled Catrin.

Catrin swung her sword against Ex Caeli Bur, as Artur continued to block her blows.

"You hold your blows because of my sex. Damn you."

"You do not need to end it this way."

"Do you think I will take pity upon Gwenhwyfawr if I kill you. My lord, defend yourself for if I lay a fatal blow, she shall surely die."

Suddenly Artur turns from defence to attack.

"Then you leave me no choice."

Queen Catrin also appeared reinvigorated as the intensity of the fight became one of life or death. Yet Artur was no match for the agility or the speed of Catrin and as he misses a thrust, she plunged her sword into his side.

Artur fell to a mass collective gasp by all those watching. Catrin suddenly rushed over, and kneeled next to him.

"My Lord and King, please forgive me."

"Spare Gwenhwyfawr."

"I cannot."

With that, Queen Catrin raised her sword towards the battlements and from afar Earin plunged his sword into Gwenhwyfawr.

"No!"

Catrin turned upon the shout of Artur to be caught by the blade of Ex Caeli Bur driven into her chest, causing her to fall on top of him as if they be in embrace, their faces touching.

Artur now dead and Catrin dying, she gently kissed his lips, before turning her head into his and closing her eyes in death.

Gwynedd and several others of the troops approached and removed the body of Catrin from on top of Artur.

Gwynedd gently recovered Ex Caeli Bur from the grip of Artur and held it aloft.

"Attack! Attack!"

Like the great roar of the fiercest storm and ocean, the mass of troops descend upon the battlements and doors to the castle, climbing them with ladders and smashing them in pure rage.

"No prisoners. Let no stone remain standing upon this most cursed of places."

****

Glastonbury

The bodies of King Artur and Queen Gwenhwyfawr were lowered into a stone lined grave at Glastonbury. Gwynedd Lancelot and the surviving kings and thousands of troops, people and priests looking on.

"Though there be war again, between Celt and Celt, let us here remember not which divides us but that which unites us," he said.

A handful of Dirt was thrown into the grave before a great team of men moved the stone lid into place.

"One day, the name of our Holly and Universal Kingdom shall return, when our people remember who they are; when they rise above the corruptions and fears of those who seek to enslave them. Until that time, we here upon the first Union of Wales remain true to this cause and I be not your king, but a prince in service."

Mercia

The lid of the tomb was finally locked into place against the other stones.

"Pray thee Pilgrim for the noble souls of Artur and Gwenhwyfawr, united once more here in peace. First King of all Great Britain. First faithful servant of the Vicar of Christ and Universal Church. Let all men who seek rule, be measured according to thy virtue. Amen."

www.ingramcontent.com/pod-product-compliance
Lightning Source LLC
Chambersburg PA
CBHW082248120626
46555CB00009B/3004